The Little Axes of Destiny

By W.R. Woodbury

Author's Biography

W.R. Woodbury was born and grew up in western Canada and from a young age had a desire to see more of the world. He has lived and worked in England, Germany, Spain, Greece and Australia and recently taken up writing again after retiring from a late career as a hotel manager in Victoria BC.

His working life has encompassed such professions as bank clerk, librarian, forestry worker, draftsman, taxi driver, highway surveyor, gardener, tour guide, house cleaner, hotel night auditor and delivery driver. During breaks in his writing life he has taken forays into painting and photography.

.

About the Book

A collection of fictional stories set in Canada, Greece, France and Australia. From an aging rock musician, to a philosophy professor, to a rancher, a bisexual married man, and a vaccination averse mother, the people in these stories reveal their strengths and weaknesses as they pass unaware through unique axis points in their lives. The choices they make will affect their destinies, whether they realize it at the time or not. The stories in this collection cover a range of topics from rivalry, to murder, sex, transformation, suicide, infidelity, domestic violence, authority, criminal justice, and the nature of love.

The stories in this collection were written in 2019, and first published online in 2020

Table of Contents

Picasso's Last Stand

Pablo's house is high above the glittering shores of the French Riviera, hidden in a hilltop forest of pines, tall olives, and red bark arbutus. The road up to it veers off the hectic Croisette, through villages of bakers, butchers, and bricolage, and swings around tight switchbacks that bring Grace Kelly to mind. Flashes of light through the trunks of the pines reveal tantalizing vistas of the shiny Mediterranean under a violet and orange evening sky.

As we near Pablo's place, scents of jasmine and rosemary spill over rough-hewn walls, which squeeze the pale, patched, asphalt lane into a single track. On either side of the road, scrubby driveways dart off to unseen houses until at the end of the crude pavement, our rental car comes to a triple intersection with four ornate gateposts. Pablo has no intention of advertising his presence but I happen to know that the way to his house is via the middle road, between the posts, up the drive with no number. After a short bumpy ride, we ease slowly over a new concrete entrance with expensive spiked iron gates that are already open. As our car approaches the house, its wheels crunch so loudly on the deep gravel of the drive that it could be a burglar alarm. We stop beside a silver BMW that is parked at the back of the house.

I know from the woman who renovated the structure, that the multi-level pale ochre farmhouse with its slate blue shutters had been more rubble than habitable building when she had come along to rescue it. With French language skills that Pablo didn't have, she had bargained for original beams from other ruins, scoured nearby villages for rustic tiles, brought in truckloads of stones and concrete. She tiled the roof in terracotta and added a round faux mill tower. The narrow house, which rises to a second floor in the centre to allow for a generous upstairs bedroom balcony, is a series of interconnecting rooms that descend the natural slope of the land toward the pool, beyond which the forest creates a jagged black outline against the darkening sky. Ghostly white oleander, blue agave, and thin dark Italian cypresses define the meandering steps that lead down to the pool. In front of the parking area at the top, a wisteria draped colonnaded boule court shows signs of recent uprooting from a herd of wild boars. Across from the kitchen entrance is a walled square pond planted with papyrus and lily-pads and stocked with koi. Three artfully placed boulders hide pump equipment because the real purpose of the étang is to serve as a reservoir in case of forest fires, and fires do rage through those hills.

Pablo's wife Sandrine, who must have heard the car on the drive, is at the oak and iron banded kitchen door to welcome us. It is a cool evening, so her small square shoulders are wrapped in a black shawl embroidered with life-sized peonies. There are no American open armed greetings for us, though she does nod and raise herself on tiptoe to accept a kiss on each cheek. We have been invited there not only for dinner, but because Pablo's agent has convinced him that he needs updated photos for marketing material. Night is not the best time for photos, but Pablo doesn't care. He is disdainful of sales techniques and doesn't need the money, so I suspect his ego has overridden his prejudices and agreed to the project. He has carried on creating music but doesn't perform concerts with his old group anymore. There are brief bursts of interest in his compositions if they are used for films or television, but these days he is more interested in creating aural landscapes. It doesn't matter whether they sell or not.

Pablo has consented to the photos only if I take them. We have known each other for twenty years, since the day the mother of his children invited me, a young untried photographer, to dinner in their London house to produce a series of family portraits. Pablo, whose real name is Paul, had acquired the nickname Picasso from the band mates in art school who had teased him about the cyclops-eyed, thick-thighed paintings he was doing at the time. Only the first name Pablo had stuck. Because I had known him for so long, we had an easy rapport, and his wife Sandrine approved of me, something she may not have done if my companion was female. Other women were a threat to her. As much as she didn't trust them, she trusted her husband less.

We planned to use his studio beside the pool for our after-dinner photo session. Pablo had suggested the location because he preferred its modern look to the rustic hand-painted Provencal décor of the house. Sometimes he slept on the sofa at the studio if he was working late, but when he did so, Sandrine complained that she worried all night. "I do it to irritate her," he once confessed.

"Gentlemen." Sandrine directs us through the small, tiled kitchen that is hung with utensils and heavy with tantalizing odours, and down a few steps to the dining area. Below that is the living room with its overstuffed brown leather furniture facing a mantled marble fireplace wide and tall enough to drive a 2CV into. Pablo's Bosendorfer baby grand is set up beside a double pair of French doors and is prominently lit from above as if he has just been playing. I am startled when he jumps up from the sofa because I hadn't noticed him sitting there with his back to us. His brown balding head had blended into the furniture and the terracotta floor tiles. He is not a tall man even standing up, so I am not surprised that seated, he has passed under my radar.

"Douglas!" he hustles his stocky frame around the floating Javanese window shutter that is the coffee table and gives me a hug. He doesn't know my partner well, so they only shake hands. "Welcome to the old man's castle." His eyes are shining at the pleasure of having company. "Sandrine, be a dear," he says, "and bring us a Pernod." He assumes that everyone wants what he does. If his guests protest, he is solicitous and apologetic, but if they show any hesitation, he makes up their minds for them. Sandrine nods like she is taking orders at a restaurant and backs away from us. When I say "thank you", she shoots me a disappointed look like I have misunderstood the rules, then tilts her chin up, turns and scuttles off like a wind-up soldier with a tight spring.

"She's a dear our Sandrine. You should get yourself one," he says, unable to resist a dig at my sexual orientation. He has been a serial and often concurrent consumer of women his whole life. It is remarkable that he had once stayed with one of them long enough to father a couple of children. It was that mother, a friend of mine, who years earlier had organized the purchase and refurbishment of the French house. At the time, Pablo was infuriated with the tax office because they wanted ninety percent of his earnings, so he took the advice of his accountant and moved to France in protest. The weather was better, and since the world became smaller every year, he saw no reason to live in England where he was born, so he stayed on far beyond the original plan.

"Drinks!" Pablo shouts toward the kitchen, but he has no sooner spoken when Sandrine bustles past the dining table and down the steps to the living room, carrying a tray of tinkling gold rimmed glasses in both hands.

"Sorry Monseigneur," she says to each of us as she passes the tray around. She has removed her shawl to reveal that she is wearing a man's shirt, probably Pablo's, tucked into an ankle length skirt, under which the red pom-poms of Egyptian slippers bobble with every step. "I had to take the time," she says. "Dinner is almost ready." Pablo has bragged that she is one of the best cooks in the south of France. Her mother still works in the family restaurant where Sandrine grew up, but she has other talents. Along with her prowess in the kitchen, she is fiercely loyal, and jealously protective of her husband. People call her "the guard dog" behind her back.

Pablo says he is not a jealous person, though none of the women he has lived with for any significant time have put him to the test. They always leave him before he leaves them. He is more possessive of his music and his cars than he is of the women in his life, so he sometimes plays them off against each other. I had heard him on occasion, tease Sandrine about her insecurities, telling her she had a big nose, that nobody else would want her, and that she was just a poor paysanne like her mother who was put on this earth to serve men like him.

When the mother of Pablo's children left him, he started drinking too much and ended up in the papers a few too many times. For the next twenty years he stumbled around Europe going from one disastrous love story to another and keeping up a double life of performing and partying until a health scare lowered his crest a few notches. When he came to earth at the French house, Sandrine was hired to cook and clean for him. It hadn't

16

taken long for her to go from being a day worker, to staying in the servant's quarters, to marrying Pablo. Their sleeping arrangements weren't obvious, and I didn't ask. Although they were married, Sandrine was officially Pablo's employee, so her social code dictated that he was her superior, a master of sorts, even though he was a foreigner. From habit she called him "Monseigneur" and to the shock of his more conventional visitors, he accepted the title. "I am a democratic person," he would say. "She can call me whatever she wants."

Once Sandrine has stopped ferrying dishes from the kitchen to the dining table, she calls out in a practiced cheery voice, "A la table!" and claps her hands together below her waist as if she is summoning a flock of chickens. Pablo takes his place at the head of the scarred and polished oak table. Sandrine sits to his right, attentive to his every need before she takes anything for herself.

The dinner conversation is all about him and he is in a talkative mood, telling stories I have never heard before. "I didn't tell her I already had a girlfriend at home," he says. "I thought the missus was away at her mum's, so when we got home an almighty catfight broke out. I let them go at it. Most fun I'd had in ages."

Sandrine sits through his storytelling with a pained half smile, pretending that she doesn't understand enough English to be embarrassed by the antics of her husband's past.

Although I have come to get photos, it has been hinted at that I might provide an appropriate quote to add to the liner notes, but I doubt I can include most of what he is telling me. Our respective partners are polite enough not to interrupt him, though I suspect he is trying to goad Sandrine. When she stands up to clear plates, my partner also gets up to help her.

"No, no, no. Please. It is mine." She sidesteps the length of the table with her back to the kitchen wall.

"I insist," my partner says, picking up a few more plates from the table. He was once a waiter, so he knows what he is doing.

"No. Please. Monsieur." Sandrine puts down the plates she has in her hand to take away the ones my partner is already carrying. "It is for me to do. Please

Monsieur." He sits down unwillingly, foiled in his attempt to get away from the awkwardness at the table.

I take the opportunity to raise the subject of photographs, hoping that the enthusiasm that Pablo has exhibited in his memories of happier times will carry over into the images. I need something other than the scowling street face he usually puts on.

"Let's go down to the studio," he says. "More space there. And I can't abide that awful din of washing up." He stares pointedly at Sandrine who has come back to carry away more dishes.

"But I have prepared a blancmange au citron," she says.

"Later." Pablo waves her away.

While I assemble my camera and lighting equipment, Pablo busies himself by sniff-testing one cigar after another from a humidified cedar cabinet in the living room.

Darkness is complete outside until Pablo turns on the garden lights. Shaded lamps hidden at the bases of trees and under retaining-wall cornices, discreetly illuminate the way down to the pool and studio. The studio is a three-sided box, the same dimensions as the pool, with a front wall of floor-to-ceiling glass. Movable soundproof barriers divide the large open interior space, and a collection of electronic keyboards fill the corners of the room. An impressive selection of guitars on stands are clustered around a drum kit that has been set up in the centre of the room. Pablo parks himself in one of the easy chairs that are grouped in a front corner near the window. With his back to his instruments and face illuminated from the shimmering glow of the turquoise pool water, I manage a few good shots before he gets bored with my instructions. He is rescued by Sandrine who arrives with coffee, though nobody has asked for it. I am not happy with the interruption, but Pablo's face brightens when she arrives, like something wakes up in him when she walks into the room.

"Leave the coffee," he says. "Go get us a brandy."

"You're not sending her all the way back up to the house?" I ask.

"There's a bar by the pool," he says. "If she hasn't stocked it up, then she's going back to the house."

"We have," Sandrine gestures toward the pool house and bows out of the room taking the coffee on a tray with her.

"Why do you treat her like a servant?" I ask, at risk of spoiling any new photo opportunities.

"Because she is. But she does it for love."

"You sleep with her though. She should be your equal," I venture, knowing that this is my own American conceit.

"Equal in what?" he asks. "Men and women are not equal, they are different." I snap a few more photos because he looks defiant.

"She's not a lesser creature than you," I try.

"Ah but she is. She knows and accepts that. And she is happy with her place."

"Have you asked her how she feels about it?"

"Why?" he puffs on his cigar. "She will tell me if she is unhappy and I will decide what to do about it."

Sandrine returns with the brandy and glasses, again assuming that everyone will drink what Pablo drinks. When she is sure that we have what we need she sits on the floor at the side of Pablo's chair with her head close to one of his knees. I snap a few more photos as we talk, and he idly strokes her hair like she is a pet animal. Soon she bends her head over his knee, exposing her exceptionally long white neck. He caresses the side of her face, smoothes and twists her long dark hair that flows loose across his lap. With his free hand he rolls his lit cigar between surprisingly long fingers and talks about the inspiration for his latest music. When he gets up to bring something to show me, Sandrine doesn't get up with him, but scoots back against the wall like she is a child who had been let into the room by special permission but doesn't want to draw attention to herself.

When Pablo sits down in his chair again, she moves back to her place by his feet and again he strokes her head like she is a favourite dog. Not once does she look at me as she plays out the ritual with her master. It makes me wonder who is the owner of whom.

The peace doesn't last beyond our second glass of brandy because Pablo takes it into his head to demonstrate how in the early days, he and his band mates dragged some groupies through a motel room window on a tour date in Arizona. Sandrine ignores his undignified antics and has retreated again with her back to the wall. She sits motionless with her gaze fixed on a back corner of the room like she is a toy that was switched off when Pablo pushed her aside so he could be the centre of attention. With his short square body, tanned bald head and fine halo of bright white hair, loud and loose print shirt, baggy shorts and bare feet, he capers around his studio like the real late-age Picasso just down the road in Mougins.

We should have left at the height of his enthusiasm because another glass of brandy tips him into an aggressive phase. I call it his Irish mood.

"What the fuck are you looking at?" he shouts at Sandrine, who as far as I can see is not looking at anything in particular. She lowers her head. "I've fucked so many women you can't even count that high." He paces the room like a barrel-chested Mussolini in a bad temper, determined to destroy something.

Sandrine stands up, puts on her shawl, and begins collecting things to take back to the main house.

"Leave the fucking glasses!" He grabs back one of them that she already has in her hand. I think it is best to pack away my camera equipment because although our evening might go on, any photos I take now won't be suitable for publication. Sandrine retreats up the path to the main house, but after a few minutes she is back with a thick hand-knitted sweater. "The night air," she says and hands it timidly to Pablo.

"You're not my fucking mother!" He tears the proffered sweater from her hands and flings it out the sliding glass door onto the pool apron. With the river of dark hair that frames her face, the carefully shaped eyebrows on her pale Celtic skin, the long straight nose and innocent lips on a wide mouth, Sandrine is like a harem odalisque, eyes brimming with tears. My photographer's eye itches to take her photo, but it is an entirely inappropriate moment. She retreats from the studio.

Pablo pours himself another brandy and I leave him there with my partner while I pack the first load of equipment up the path to the car. The house lights are on when I get up to the house, but there is nobody in sight. I step into the kitchen and call Sandrine's name. The dishes in the kitchen are neatly stacked to dry, the table in the dining room is clear, and there is silence in the rest of the house. As I stow my gear in the back at the car, I hear Pablo and my partner talking and laughing as they make halting progress up the steps. When I stand up, I think I can see their shadows approaching the koi pond.

The dark and perfumed night air is unexpectedly punctured by a scream, followed by muffled screeches and a man's voice so loud and angry that it alarms me. As I run down the path toward the commotion, I hear the woman's voice rise to a wail. When I get there Pablo is holding a long butcher knife in one hand.

"The bitch tried to kill me," he says. The woman lunges at him to take the weapon away from him, but my partner holds her arms behind her back. In the gloom I can see there is blood running down Pablo's arm, though he appears not to notice. "Crazy salope!" he shouts at her. "You can't knock off this old fucker just like that."

Sandrine falls to her knees and kisses his feet. "Forgive me Monseigneur," she pleads. "Forgive me. It is stronger than me." Her sobs take over from her words.

Pablo doesn't exactly kick her, but tries to raise her to her feet with his foot. "Get up." His voice is cold, sober, and angry. She embraces his legs, but he pulls away. He allows me to reach over and pry the knife from his hand. I step back a few paces, keeping the bloody blade behind me. When Sandrine notices the blood on his hand, she tries to climb up him like he is a tree. He doesn't stop her but remains motionless with his legs apart huffing like a bull. She is solicitous and apologetic and kisses his hand even though she gets blood on her lips. Pleading and pulling him by his good hand, she drags him to the kitchen to see what damage she has done.

We offer to drive him to the hospital, but he won't hear of it. He is happy with the tape and gauze wrap that

Sandrine has improvised to stop the flow of blood. "I'll take a painkiller and if it's still bad tomorrow I'll see a doctor," he says.

Once we are sure no more harm will be done, we steer our exhausted way down the dimly lit, tree-shrouded lanes until we come out to the welcoming lights of Cannes with its naked transvestites under long fur coats doing a brisk trade on the Croisette.

When I call Pablo a few weeks later to say that I have finished the first edit on the photos, I ask him how his hand is. "Of course, we kissed and made up," he says. "Now she is putty in my hands," he laughs.

"That's nothing new," I venture, but he lets it go. He wants to see the photos in person because he expects to be signing autographs on them and he wants to choose the most flattering images of himself.

It is a hot mid morning in August when I pull up onto the drive, and immediately spot Pablo sitting on the wall of the étang in the sun, feeding Cheerios to the koi.

"How's the hand?" I ask, seeing that it is still bandaged.

"It was the Victorinox," he says. "They're excellent knives." He turns his hand over and over to show me, but the wound is well hidden by bandages.

"Is Sandrine still here? You didn't send her packing, did you?" It would be just like him to throw her out in a fit of temper even though she was his wife. He has never told me in so many words that they are married, and he has never called her his wife in my company. I already know the true state of affairs from his children's mother. As his son and daughter had neared the age of majority, their mother made noises about their inheritance, so Pablo immediately married Sandrine to make sure that the illegitimate children, and by proxy their mother, never got their hands on any of his considerable loot. The yellow press had often carried stories about his money and his women, but they had missed Sandrine because they didn't know about the marriage. She was a servant who did the shopping, and she was French, so presumably wouldn't have any influence at all on the great English maestro. Pablo had been married once before at twenty, at a time that coincided with the first temptations of fame, but when his young wife died of an overdose, he never married again, not even to the mother of his children, not until Sandrine. I vaguely remembered stories about his young first wife attracting his attention by stabbing herself in the hand at a restaurant table, but I didn't dare bring it up in case he used it as fuel to torment Sandrine.

"Of course, she's here." He sounds surprised I'd ask. "She needs some poor bastard like me to satisfy her Mother Teresa complex." He closes the Cheerio box and leads the way to the kitchen. Sandrine is at the counter with her back to us and when she turns, I see that she has the same Victorinox in her hand and it is pointed at me. A few green flakes of parsley fall to the floor, but she doesn't notice. Her eyes have a faraway glazed look, and when I spot a half empty glass of red wine on the counter, I step back a pace, wondering if she might poke the knife into my guts. Maybe she has been sparring with her husband again.

"Don't worry." Pablo steps between us and pushes the knife aside with his bandaged hand. "She has already done all of the damage she wants." He kisses her on the cheek, and we leave the kitchen to let her carry on with the parsley, but I can't help keeping one eye over my shoulder.

I spread the photos out on the dining table so Pablo can walk around them and select the best ones. For a photographer it is difficult to understand the reasons people have for liking a particular image of themselves over another. They look too old or too young, too thin, or too fat. They don't like their chin, mouth, nose, or eyes. They look like their brother or sister, mother, or father, crazy or sad. Pablo is no different, but by luck, his choices and mine intersect at a few places so we agree to use the mutually selected photos. For him it is a quick and reasoned process, a step that needs taking, like choosing the right note in a composition. He is an artist who doesn't waste time agonizing; choices need to be made if a piece is ever to be finished. Considering his vanity, I am surprised by how quickly he made his selection.

"That was easy," I say, impressed by his clear-headed artistic commitment. My compliments are forgotten when he claps his hands like a child at a birthday party and calls out, "Champagne!"

Sandrine is immediately at the kitchen door, drying her hands on her apron.

"I said I would wait until we had finished this and now, we are done," Pablo says and puffs out his chest like a rooster looking for approval.

"Peut-être un bébé," Sandrine says.

"Non mon cher." His sweetness is halfway between genuine and sarcastic. "Not un bebe. A full bottle of bub. To celebrate with my friend."

"But the antibiotics Monseigneur?"

"Fuck the antibiotics woman," he gestures her away like a bee that has tried to enter the room. "Just bring the damn bottle!"

"Maybe she's right," I say. "You shouldn't."

His eyes narrow. "Don't you go against me too," he says.

As I gather the photos into a pile, he pulls out one that is of him and Sandrine where she is sitting at his feet while he strokes her hair.

"I can keep this for myself?" he asks and briefly flashes it at me.

"Of course," I answer. "Whatever you like."

Sandrine has come back with a frosty bottle of champagne and two flutes, so Pablo quickly tucks the photo he intends to keep under my briefcase, which is lying flat on the table.

"Leave it out on the terrace," he points toward the patio doors. When she has returned to the kitchen, he retrieves the hidden photo and tucks it into a book in the living room, giving me a mischievous wink though I am not entirely sure what I am supposed to understand.

As we sit and clink glasses out on the edge of the garden, a chorus of humming bees and distant cicadas surrounds us. He tells me that the tendons Sandrine has cut might take a long time to heal. "I still can't move most of the fingers on my left hand, so I'm not the same keyboard whiz I used to be. I don't know that I will ever get it back. You might say my wings have been clipped."

"Did you have any dates coming up?"

"Nothing important. Nothing I need. Hate going out anyway." He pours us another flute. "And she wants us to have a baby." He tilts his head toward the kitchen, so it is clear we are talking about Sandrine. "She's trying to get me healthy," he says, "so I can produce a miniature monster version of myself."

"Are you going to do it?" I ask. "You've already got two."

He stands up with his glass in hand and indicates that we walk down through the garden to the pool. The sun is hot overhead, but the umbrella pines scattered through the property, make islands of dappled shade to linger beneath. The stone steps widen as we near the pool deck where the cerulean blue water is perfectly still and inviting.

Pablo seats us in the shade of the pool cabana.

"I never liked the kids' mother," he says. "She's a grasping type, always wants more, too independent. Why would she go for a man like me except for the money? She tried to change me, but it didn't work. We were like billy goats butting heads the whole time."

"But your children shouldn't suffer because you don't like their mother."

"They are the same as her. I can see it in them already. They'll be happy to pick my bones clean when I'm gone."

Just then Sandrine appears at the bottom of the garden steps and walks onto the pavement surrounding the pool. She trails a towel in her hand, has a wide sunhat on her head, and is wearing a skin-tight one-piece swimsuit that makes her look more naked than dressed. She pretends not to see us. We watch her without speaking and though she does nothing unusual, her movements are too slow and exaggerated to be innocent. She is not tall but is perfectly proportioned with abundant breasts, an hourglass waist, and muscular ballerina's thighs. She walks out on the low diving board, does a few stretches so we can see her magnificent body, before she stands on tiptoe and executes a perfectly simple swan dive. She remains submerged for longer than I think is healthy, and I wonder if she has underestimated the depth, but then her head breaks the surface and she breaststrokes her way over to us. When she puts her tanned arms up on the edge of the pool, her hair is slicked back and her long dark eyelashes drip with residual water. A few sunspots have freckled her noble nose.

"Fuck," Pablo's voice is slurred, perhaps from the champagne.

"I'd better be going," I say and stand up to look for whatever belongings I have brought with me, only to realize that all I have is the glass in my hand. I consider taking it up to the house with me, but it isn't empty, so I put it down again to avoid last minute orders to the contrary from Pablo. He doesn't say goodbye; he isn't the most polite of men. The usually solicitous Sandrine doesn't notice my exit either, and continues to fix Pablo with her alluring eyes, in full possession of herself, her man, and her household.

Grief Takes A Holiday

"She comes every year," Phaedra said. "The first time was with her husband maybe ten years ago, but he died." She made the Orthodox sign of the cross and kissed her thumb against her closed fist. She bestowed her Christian gesture of blessing not only on the dead, but used it indiscriminately to keep bad luck away, wagging her head as if to say, there but for the grace of God go I.

Phaedra and her married son owned a restaurant on the small beach where I sometimes ate a late dinner. The restaurant was named after Phaedra's dead husband Alexis, but the building had once been her father's boathouse, so it had been passed down to her. She rented rooms up in the village, spare rooms in an empty family house that would go to waste if they weren't rented for extra income. The English Woman always stayed with Phaedra.

The local children whispered and laughed when the visitor passed by. They hopped behind her like chimpanzees, pulling down their eyelids with sticky fingers, hardly able to believe that such a creature existed and now they were seeing one for real. Even adults did double takes, unable to curb their instincts to stop and gawk before they smiled weakly and moved on.

Every morning, in a light cotton sundress with a floral bag slung over her shoulder, the tall woman galumphed down the hill on her way to the beach. Her sandals slapped the pavement and her tapered tree trunk legs vibrated as each foot hit the ground. Her stride was necessarily long because she was more than two meters tall. She was also splay footed and on the downhill as she gained momentum, her body pitched perilously forward, and her feet kicked out to each side in a blind search for temporary pivots to support the ungainly creature they were carrying.

The few evenings of the week when I ate inside the restaurant, she sat alone at a table out on the terrace. More than her height, I was struck by her important manly nose that should have been on a stronger head. Her long jaw hosted a full and fleshy lower lip and a thin upper one that was almost swallowed by the pout of the lower one. Her watery shimmering blue eyes were like the reflection on a mountain lake except that they were red rimmed, afire on the shores. One eye was more difficult to read as it had a permanent squint as if from pain. The other was wide and staring, on the verge of being horrified. A thick head of sandy blonde hair was strictly parted and pulled back into a bun.

"Poor thing," Phaedra dried her hands on her apron. "I suppose we shouldn't pity her because she comes back all the time; but she suffers. When I lost my first husband, his empty shadow followed me everywhere." She sighs, crosses herself again and mutters something only meant to be understood by God or Alexis, and goes back to the endless dishes in the kitchen.

On previous evenings Phaedra had filled me in on what she knew about the tall woman. She had apparently been single well into her thirties. "Very old," Phaedra said. Then she met an Englishman who was on holiday. When they came back the next year it was for their honeymoon. Phaedra was proud to say that they had met at her restaurant and she fawned over them like they were prodigal children who had come home. For a few years, the couple arrived at the beginning of June when the jasmine bloomed and stayed at Phaedra's house up in the village. They ate at her restaurant, and never missed a sunset, sitting side by side in folding chairs pulled out onto the beach, barefoot in the sand, holding hands and hardly speaking. When they missed a year nobody knew why, until the next year when the tall woman arrived alone. Her husband had a heart attack at work and didn't make it to the hospital in time.

"I can imagine her world," Phaedra said. It was the end of the evening; the woman had just left the restaurant and Phaedra was taking her time changing the paper tablecloths. "When I lost my Alexi, I sat around home all day thinking about ending my life, but that would be a sin." She crossed herself to show God that she hadn't been serious about her desire to end things. "I thought I'd go crazy but then I had my boy to look after so I had to get to work." With the old paper tablecloths scrunched against her chest, she shuffled off to the kitchen in her sandaled feet, the day's tracked-in beach sand making a soft shoe rhythm on the terrazzo tiles as she walked.

Later we watched the tall woman make her way up the hill. She swayed when she walked and placed one foot deliberately in front of the other like she was climbing a ladder. Every once in a while she would stop and hug herself, and I imagined when I saw her broad back shake, that she was crying. When she started off again it was with a big slow step, like the first foot on a pilgrimage, and then she heaved the other side of her body forward, finding her pace like an ox at the wheel, but every twenty steps she would stop again and her shoulders would droop. Phaedra insisted that she wasn't drunk. "Two small glasses of ouzo, I swear that's all."

The next afternoon I stopped by the restaurant earlier than usual because I had to deliver tickets to one of the tour boats that stopped at the jetty. As I started back up the hill, I noticed the English woman in the turquoise water of the bay below. She was standing up to her waist, surrounded by a group of young boys, splashing and laughing. Her hair had fallen half out of its chignon, and her head was tilted back with the playful innocence of a Picasso bather.

I had never seen her in a bathing suit. Her two-piece baby-doll costume was large enough to be modest but eccentrically out of style with its pink cotton ruffles on the top and bottom. Like her legs, her body was almost without shape, like an eight-year-olds, cranked up to giant size. The tanned boys in their dark shorts surrounded the tall pale woman, splashing and circling, moving closer and then pinwheeling their arms backwards to get away when she almost touched them. She may not have realized that she was the centre of a circle, which to me looked like the makings of a feeding frenzy.

The boys splashed and fell over, spit water and came up laughing. The woman splashed them back, laughing and jumping up and down with them, lost in joy for a moment, though her stiff movements betrayed a hint of embarrassed indulgence. She splashed her long arms on the surface of the water sending out concentric waves, and for a moment she was like a child experimenting with her first immersion in the sea. When the older boys moved closer to her she splashed and squealed to keep them at bay. As she bounced up and down in the sea, I saw her expression relax into a sort of blissful ecstasy as she anticipated the waves that caressed hidden parts of her body. At the height of the group's excitement, the tallest boy in the group, not really a boy anymore, approached her slowly and reached one hand out toward her. In the noise and splashing she didn't notice his stillness at first but when she did, she stopped laughing and fixed her eyes on him. Her hands were underwater, and she swirled them in coy circles from back to front, as out of breath, huffing and smiling, she gave the young man a shy smile. He reached out his hand again and shook it as if to say, "Take it." She lowered her eyes like a demure lady whose hand has been requested by a knight, a lady who is too shy to admit she wants it too. When the young man slapped the flat of his hand on the water to make a noisy splash, she looked up and stretched out a long trembling hand as if to calm him. He took her by the wrist and pulled her away from the group into shallower water and escorted her across the beach to the restaurant. He gestured for her to sit down at one of the tables, but he remained standing, so they were eye to eye. She said something to him; he nodded slowly and walked away.

The tall woman continued to frequent the beach every day but in the last week of her holiday she had taken to leaving before sunset. I noticed that her progress up the hill at the end of the day had changed character. The hill was a struggle for anyone, but recently the widow made the trip up to the village without stopping, with a determined positivity rather than with the once painful Stations of the Cross.

Early one morning I happened to be in the village square when the local bus left for the airport. It was hard to miss the tall woman in the gaggle of travelers who waited for the bus doors to open. She was tanned and relaxed, at peace with herself, and in the crowd had not backed away into her usual invisibility. When she put a foot onto the first step of the bus, she knocked her head on the top of the door because she was distracted by waving at someone on the other side of the square. I looked over expecting to see Phaedra, but instead caught a glimpse of a young man who immediately ducked behind a taller man's shoulder. I looked back at her in time to see her blow a kiss in a different direction and noticed the young man again, already halfway out of the square with his head down like none of this had anything to do with him.

It is true that the world is shrinking. That winter I needed to fly to London to renew some documents and it took less than a day to travel from the tiny village on the Mediterranean to a friend's house in Islington. The next day I took the tube to the embassy and was impressed when the bureaucracy was done with me earlier than I anticipated. When I stepped back out onto Trafalgar Square, I remembered that the sprawling Portland stone building up to my left was the National Gallery. I hadn't been in there for at least ten years and since I wasn't expected home for dinner until early evening, I headed across the square to give the place another quick look. The portico was draped with coloured banners for the latest exhibition, but I didn't look at them, as I knew exactly where I wanted to go. Once inside the main entrance hall, I turned immediately right toward the Turners and Monets. I sat for a while in front of an entire wall of impressionist lily pads to calm my thoughts and summon enough interest to poke my head into a few other rooms. Back toward the entrance I was swept up in a guided group shuffling toward the opposite wing, so I followed them through to an exhibition of paintings by Da Vinci. There were portraits of young men and portraits of women; the Lady with an Ermine had a knot of whispering Germans in front of her. Moving a few rooms along, feeling oppressed by the dark masterpieces and looking for an exit, I noticed the tall widow standing in the middle of the room, a few steps back from a crowd in front of the The Virgin of the Rocks. Two versions of the painting were on display, the gallery's copy and one from the Louvre, but I was more interested in the tall woman than comparing the details of the adjacent masterpieces. I glanced over as often as I dared without drawing attention though I was sure she wouldn't recognize me. It happens that we encounter people we know from another context, and we are not sure if we know them or not, and are reluctant to approach, but I was sure it was her. There weren't many like her in the world, but what put me off track at first was that this woman was very pregnant, at the full bloom stage when the hormones have kicked in to give the expectant mother a halo of radiance, and the child a fighting chance of survival.

I sat down with my back to the crowd as if I was interested in a Raphael Madonna on the other wall, but it gave me an opportunity to study her surreptitiously. Her luxuriant crimped and wavy fair hair was spread across her shoulders like Leonardo's Salvator Mundi, She wore a sleeveless flowered dress that did little to hide the beach ball bump in front, and a v-necked dress showing a developing cleavage, plumping up soft and milky for the baby. The short dress revealed that her knees were still childish, but her calves were showing some curves instead of the straight legs that had posted her along with such ungainliness. Maybe the shape was helped by the exercise of carrying extra weight or by the lipstick red clogs on her feet that forced her calves to do more work. A small red leather bag was slung over her shoulder and the same colour was picked up on her lips. An expert cosmetic hand had reshaped her mouth, so it looked more natural, the top lip more balanced with the bottom. Her face glowed with the assurance of a creature who is about to fulfill a higher purpose. When she tilted her head back to shake the hair off her shoulders, her important nose looked aristocratic and regal rather than simply large. Even in the dim light I could see that she had the same shimmering blue eyes but that a light touch of mascara and eyeliner had turned their watery sadness into something as feminine and mystical as an Egyptian pharaoh. Fanning herself with an exhibition guide, she looked from one painting of the Virgin to its neighbour as if she were watching a tennis match. Occasionally she took a step forward to study a detail but knowing that nobody could see the paintings if she was in front, she politely returned to the back row.

As always, she attracted stares, but people were less inclined to treat her like a circus freak when they noticed that she was pregnant. If she moved close to a group, they parted like the Red Sea. People stared at her but rather than hide from them as I had seen her do, she smiled and nodded, pretending that everything was as it should be in spite of her towering height. As much as the change in her physical appearance was obvious, she had a new presence that was based on recently acquired self-assurance. The robotic movements that I remembered were now smoothly connected, as if her body had finally figured out how all its parts fitted together. I was surprised when she pulled a small mirror out of her purse to check the state of her lipstick. As she pouted and turned one way then the other, I realized that I had never seen her show any sign of vanity. She was someone who avoided mirrors and spent a large part of her public energy trying to disappear. Satisfied with her makeup, she snapped the mirror closed, dropped it back into her purse and turned toward the exit door. When I turned to leave the room, she looked right at me as she passed by, but I didn't see her eyes light up, though her high cheeks rose in the beginning of a smile. As she walked away her feet sounded heavily on the parquet floor and I saw that her walk had changed, that her hips moved with a new fluidity in spite of the baby bump out the front. She had gone from a loose assemblage of shapeless pre-pubescent limbs and torso to the confident queen of her own anima.

I waited until she had left the room and then hid myself behind lingering knots of people as I surreptitiously headed for the entrance door. She was well ahead of me, but her height made her difficult to miss. I was disappointed when she folded herself into a black cab. I wanted to know more, but it was not in my nature to run after her and introduce myself. I had no right to crash into her life, so I stood on the top of the wide flight of stone steps of the gallery watching her be driven away, wondering if the baby had been conceived on her last holiday. I calculated that her visit was seven months ago, so it seemed highly likely. I hoped that she wouldn't go back. She should take her new life and run with it; to start over like there was no past. The young man wasn't ready; he would deny her.

Grief had once dropped into her garden and stood around like a granite headstone with its mouth open, swallowing the untethered parts of her soul. It was a solid little monument that she had muscled aside to tidy the scenery, but it would never disappear. For the moment it was forgotten because a new life was calling, but every life was fragile, and the gritty stone would always be nearby collecting dust until the next time the wind blew.

The Threshing Floor

Teddy strapped a packsaddle onto a reliable bay mare to carry salt and mineral blocks up to the Herefords that grazed on the high forest grass during summer. He saddled the mare's filly for himself and nodded at the dogs who had been wagging their tails fast and low, hoping they would be allowed to run along with him and sniff the exotic smells in the wild world.

The afternoon's destination was a salt lick in a clearing at the top of the ridge that separated the main ranch from the original homestead his grandparents had built in a lower valley. Teddy's father had kept the old property for its field of clover and timothy that was mowed for its one sweet crop in August. Most of the family's herd and wealth was scattered across multiple grazing leases fifty miles south of the ranch, and in winter the animals were crowded into muddy feedlots close to town for easy auction and transport. Prize breeders and sentimental specimens over-wintered up at the home ranch.

From the salt lick at the top of the ridge, the only part visible of the abandoned place below was the tip of a promontory behind the homestead where the old threshing floor jutted out like a thumb over the valley below. As Teddy stood up in his stirrups to get a better look, he spotted a flash of something bright out on the point that he decided needed investigation. Rather than take the horses back home to fetch his pickup truck to drive the long way round, he reasoned that he was halfway there already so it would be quicker to ride. Nobody had been down to the place in weeks, and it never hurt to check the fences. His heels prodded the inexperienced filly toward the steep dusty trail that pitched down the hillside into the pines. He pulled back hard on the reins as they descended while his horse slid on its rear haunches, slipping a bit with every step. He needed to go slowly to keep the right tension on the rope of the packhorse behind so it had time to find its unwilling feet. Once down the steepest part he let the horses canter to snort off their nervous tension from the descent.

The pines on the ridge had given way to a dense Douglas Fir forest that blocked so much light that only weak spindly grass could grow under them. As they approached the edge of the bench-land before it swooped off into the lower valley, the narrow path opened into a two-wheel track. The horses wanted to run but Teddy held them back because directly ahead was an almost invisible barbed wire gate that led into the back of the hayfield. Year after year more white-barked aspen with their dancing leaves had sprung up around the fences at the edge of the forest. His grandfather had waged war on the invasive trees. "The damn things don't even make good kindling" he'd say. Nobody had carried his battle forward so a third generation of seedlings had crept out and filled in gaps. The original upstarts were showing dark scars of heart rot.

The border collies that ran alongside Teddy's horse leapt ahead when they sighted the open field and they squeezed under the gate before he had time to open it. They cut around the edge of the hayfield and ran toward a clump of lilac bushes where the entrance to the old house had been. As Teddy closed the gate, he noticed the dogs veer off barking toward the old threshing floor where he thought he had seen the glint of light.

Their grandfather had chosen that particular spot on the edge of the world because if he closed his eyes he could imagine the Mediterranean at his feet, though in reality it was the only location on the property with a strong reliable breeze for winnowing. The wheat field in front of the house wasn't large enough to merit a mechanical harvester. A wide-mouthed beast like a combine could not negotiate the winding switchback road up to the ranch, so he cut the fields with a horse drawn mower, stooked the sheaves by hand, and flailed the wheat on the threshing floor. His wife winnowed the grain in a shallow basket and the children were assigned to gather the kernels that got away. The family eked out a reasonable existence, trading for what they didn't have, not missing the things they didn't need, happy to live simply and independently, an existence based on the strength of their backs and their willingness to work hard every day.

Squatters had burnt down the main house on the homestead a few years earlier leaving only a scorched crumbling chimney, a burned out stove at its feet, and a robust lilac bush on either side of what had been the front door. When Teddy was a child, a farmhand and his family lived in the house. The cast iron and cream enamel stove in the kitchen was the hub of the house. It was kept alight to heat water from the well for washing and to cook meals for the hard-working family. The farmer's wife always had warm cookies for the boys.

Teddy nudged his horse to a trot after the dogs, following fresh tire tracks in the grass. He arrived in time to hear the dogs go silent and see them wag their tails as they approached a familiar open top Jeep that had skidded out onto an open area at the edge of the promontory. With a spectacular view over a series of lower valleys that marched off to the Western horizon, it was a defined circle as large as the ranch house that had once been paved in a jigsaw puzzle of interlocking slate slabs. Benches of cut logs had bracketed the stone circle but had disappeared into cook stoves over the years. Although neglected, the paving stones were still in place and remained remarkably free of vegetation.

Teddy's grandfather had been a big influence on him until he died when the boy was ten. Nobody told him at the time that his grandfather had committed suicide in the tool-shed. It took a few years of deflected questions before his mother explained that her father in law had been diagnosed with terminal cancer and couldn't face being incapacitated. Teddy also learned that his grandfather had come to Canada because he had been a socialist in a country with Mussolini on the rise. For his older brother Charles to drive his Jeep out onto the threshing floor was like driving over the grave of the old man.

The boys were two years apart. Charles had been the king of the family until his brother came along. From the beginning he demonstrated that he was not happy that he was no longer the chosen one by throwing all of his baby brother's toys down the outdoor toilet. The sons expected they would inherit what was now a considerable family empire . Although their father was only in his sixties, his back was so bent from a lifetime of wrestling with the land that he could hardly participate in the daily chores. If there were places he could drive to, he was happy to give advice but he had to leave the daily running of the business to his sons. There had been an informal division of duties that allowed them to follow their natural interests.

Teddy was responsible for livestock, and Charles was all for business and industrial agriculture. He had irrigated and planted oats and barley on the flat land the family owned in the valley bottom. The crop went to feed the cattle they kept in feedlots, but if it was a bumper year, Charles kept the profit and indulged his informal hobby of buying and wrecking vehicles.

As Teddy rode up to the side of the Jeep, Charles barely turned his head. He had watched the dogs and horses approach in his rear view mirror.

"What are you doing up here?" Teddy asked.

Charles tapped his fingers on the Jeep door. "I don't need your permission?" He was calm but unfriendly.

"I thought it was trespassers from up top. That's how we lost the old house."

"This is a shit piece of property," Charles lifted his tan straw cowboy hat and wiped the sweat from his forehead. "We should sell it."

"I don't think dad will go for that. Anyway, what's the rush?"

"You don't know anything do you?" Charles looked up with a sneer. "We need the money. Simple as that. We have to pay down the equipment loans."

"We wouldn't owe so much if you hadn't bought that top of the line stuff that was made for wide open fields in Saskatchewan."

Charles' jaw muscles clenched and relaxed. "You're too busy up here playing the cowboy," he said, "to know the first thing about business so you can go to hell with that." His fingers drummed harder on the rolled down window edge. Teddy recognized this touchy aggressive behaviour and was wary of it, as he had seen his brother's temper explode in disproportionate ways. He had a bad habit of throwing things when he was in a rage. An unexpected claw hammer had once hit Teddy in the mouth and broke one of his front teeth. In face to face disagreements, Charles would move in close to his opponent to emphasize his superior height and step into the other's space as if he wanted to bump chests like a silver-back gorilla asserting dominance. Charles was never very articulate but by thirteen he was taller and wider than both of his parents, so he usually got his way. Teddy was almost as big as his brother but wasn't as much of a force because he didn't throw his weight around.

The dogs had given up scratching at the side of the Jeep and were sniffing their way toward a lopsided log granary that was surrounded by the new growth poplars at the edge of the clearing. Charles' attention was on the dogs.

"I don't like people parking out here." Teddy said as he followed Charles' gaze and saw a young woman appear from behind the granary and straighten up her clothes. The dogs jumped excitedly around her feet.

"What's she doing here?" Teddy didn't wait for an answer but rode over to her as she walked toward them. Adele was Teddy's fiancée. They had set a date to marry next summer.

"I needed to pee," she smiled brightly up at Teddy, who dismounted and reached for her hand.

"What are you doing out with him?" he tipped his head toward his brother who had stayed in the Jeep.

"He wanted to show me this place," she said. "I've heard you talk about it."

"I would have brought you here." He leaned over to kiss her cheek, but she sidestepped him and bent over to pet the dogs.

"It's no big deal. I thought you wouldn't mind."

Teddy did mind because she didn't know his brother like he did. Given the opportunity he would try to take everything that wasn't already his, even things that he didn't want. When they were younger, Charles took Teddy's things to get a rise out of him and make it look like his younger brother was a difficult child.

"You should have asked," Teddy stroked Adele's shoulder.

"You're always busy," she put her arms around his neck. "He offered so I said yes."

Adele and Teddy had been introduced at a mutual friend's wedding. She was from a local well-known family of sheep farmers. Teddy had known of her from his boyhood days in the 4H club when he exhibited Herefords and she showed her Dorsets. Every time they got together at a springtime lambing or a cattle drive, they teased each other and laughed easily like the best of friends. Teddy's parents loved her and made remarks about producing beautiful grandchildren. In fact, Terry and Adele had started sleeping together the year before they finished high school and did so whenever they had the opportunity. They wanted children eventually but agreed to wait until they were married.

Charles honked the horn like a taxi waiting on a city street. The packhorse jumped, and a panicked grouse flapped up from the undergrowth to launch itself over the edge of the bench-land.

"Come home with me baby." Teddy dipped his face into the cascade of blonde hair on Adele's shoulder that smelled like jasmine and wind. "I'll take off the packsaddle and go bareback. You can ride mine."

"I can't," she said. "Charles's going back to town and I have to be there for a class tonight." She was studying at the local college for a degree in agriculture.

"I'd rather you didn't," Teddy said. "I know him better than you do."

"Don't worry pumpkin," she said. "I'm a big girl." She stood on her tiptoes to give him a peck on the lips and then pulled herself up into the passenger seat of the Jeep. Charles looked straight ahead as he punched the vehicle through a three point turn, spitting up pebbles and grass and giving the Jeep extra gas when he was on the dirt track so it left a cloud of dust that filled the clearing. Teddy glared at the truck as the dogs went barking after it.

As he turned his horse away from the threshing floor for the plodding ride home, he knew that his brother was trying to make him jealous on purpose. The sooner he married Adele the better. He would have liked to move their wedding closer, but Adele had set the date because she wanted to finish school. Meanwhile there were chores to do and a ranch to run, but he couldn't get the image of Adele and Charles racing down the highway, Charles driving recklessly just to scare her, playing the fool, both of them laughing. He would need to talk to his father about keeping the old homestead no matter what Charles had in mind for it.

Enderby, BC. -- A North Okanagan man died Tuesday after being sucked into a combine while working in a field in the Spallumcheen Valley. A source told law enforcement that Teddy Piccardi, 25, was trying to get the header out of a bind when he got trapped in the machine. He ended up losing both legs in the initial entrapment. His brother was with him and provided medical aid until paramedics arrived. However, Piccardi didn't survive. Because of the rough terrain, the ambulance was unable to make it to the scene of the accident. Enderby RCMP helped transport EMS workers to the scene on all-terrain vehicles

When the fallout from Teddy's death had settled to a bearable level, the parents went on a European tour to distract themselves. They visited distant cousins in Italy and in England but on the last leg at Heathrow Airport, the hardworking rancher had a heart attack and died there and then. His wife came home a couple of days late with her husband's body in a steel box.

"I would have gone to bring him back," Charles said. "But it's the wrong time of year. Dad was a rancher, so he'd know what I'm talking about. Anyway, the cost was all covered. Ma just needed to get on a plane."

The widow made it known that she didn't want anything to do with ranching ever again and retired to a small house the family bought in the city where it was easy for her to hide her increasing consumption of vodka. Charles took over the business; finally able to have free rein to expand in whatever direction he wanted. He was not interested in subsistence farming, home ranches or sentiment. Agribusiness was the future and, in a few years, by expanding his feedlots and grain production, he had quadrupled the family's finances.

On one of the few occasions that he checked on his mother, she was, as usual, several drinks into a sentimental afternoon. They sat at the kitchen table as the family always did no matter where they lived, and after stumbling over some roundabout evasions, she eventually confessed there was a family secret she thought Charles should know. "With all of the hurt that's been done it doesn't matter anymore." She swirled the ice cubes in her freshly filled glass. "It's about Teddy." She spoke without hesitation, as if she had recited the story to herself so many times that it didn't touch her anymore. "When you were little, we lived at the ranch full time. The closest neighbours, your dad's cousins, were ten miles away. Most of the day I was home with you, except when your dad came stamping around the kitchen looking for lunch or dinner. He'd come charging in, clap his hands, eat everything in sight then disappear until after dark. You were a fussy baby, you cried when your dad picked you up, and you cried all day when you were home with me."

"I gave you a lot of trouble huh," Charles laughed with pride but his mother didn't smile.

"One day when your father was out pushing cattle up the mountain," she continued, "this old Ford came rattling across the log bridge and drove right up to the garden gate. Cars didn't stop by the place very much, so I was already on the porch by the time the driver got to the front steps. He was young and beautiful, with a blonde beard. He had on a long coat and a planter's hat, not a cowboy one like everyone round here wears. I couldn't help myself. Your dad left me alone so much."

"Nothing I could have done about that," Charles said. "Dad was married to that damn place." Charles looked out the window, indifferent to the ghosts of his mother's past.

"He was so charming, a real southern gentleman, and from Carolina no less. He took off his hat and called me ma'am."

"How come you never told dad?" Charles turned an accusing eye on her.

"He thought the baby was his," she looked down at her drink. "The gentleman was lighter skinned than him, but blonde hair runs in my family. Your father didn't need to know."

Charles studied his mother as she sat at the table, looking her up and down as if recalculating his opinion of her.

"Don't you see?" She took a couple of gulps from her glass and paused to catch her breath. "It was all going to be yours anyway."

"I know that. It always was mine from the start. I'm the oldest." Charles tipped back on his kitchen chair, something his mother hated him doing because he had broken quite a few pieces of furniture that way. He was impatient with his mother's tipsy ramblings.

"You know what I mean," she muttered. "Without...without..." She sucked the last of the vodka out of her glass though the cubes hadn't melted.

Charles stood up and collected his cowboy hat from the table, kissed her on the top of the head. "You're drinking too much these days Ma." He let the screen door on its long spring slam on his way out.

Year by year his business earned more money, but Charles began to look for other things to do. He built himself a house but was alone in it. After a respectful time, he approached Adele to ask her out for an evening, but she refused the invitation and would hardly look at him as he made his proposal. "It's her loss," he told his friends. "I would have given her a helluva better life than she'd have had with Teddy."

When he wasn't at work, Charles spent most evenings at cocktail bars drinking expensive rum and buying drinks for whatever acquaintances he could assemble. Someone suggested that since he liked rum so much, he might want to go to the Caribbean. Charles thought it was too exotic, so they suggested Puerto Vallarta in Mexico instead. "You'll find plenty of women on holidays and you know what that means."

Charles ended up buying a condominium in Mexico. Every year when the last harvest was off the fields in Canada, he left the business in the hands of his manager and flew south. He was introduced to an indigenous single mother who started out as his housekeeper but moved in with him when things took a more intimate turn. She babied him like his mother, put up with his oddities, his drinking, and his absences while he was back in Canada.

The yearly commute worked for a couple of years, but he was usually reluctant to go back to Canada and spent more and more time down south. His mother died when he was in Mexico, but he didn't go back for the funeral though he had paid for it. There was nobody left to judge him so could do as he liked without anyone tut-tutting over his shoulder. When his financial adviser suggested it might be the right time to sell his property in Canada, he took the advice, invested his funds, and moved to Mexico for good. After a year of constant cohabitation his partner got fed up with him and found someone she liked better. Charles moved to Thailand looking for a similar set up but he didn't last long there either. Every time he tried to put down roots his plans came to nothing. He moved frequently but never stopped anywhere for long. His prolonged presence in any one place seemed to poison the earth under his feet.

Suppression Crew

"Don't go up there." Raphael pointed toward a bluff at the entrance to Bull Canyon where a horizontal row of caves, like the darkened entrances to a stone temple, separated the towering vertical cliff above from the spill of scree and scrub below. "It is a place sacred to my people."

Raphael the crew chief, along with four young men, was washing a pickup truck in front of a row of plywood sleeping cabins. The huts on log skids, the aluminium roofed cook shack, and a couple of lean-to garages, made up the Alexis Creek Forest Service Fire Suppression Camp. In a ravine behind the camp, the turquoise Chilcotin River had receded after the height of its spring snowmelt runoff, but still roared in the background over an obstacle course of white boulders.

"Too bad." Owen looked around for support. "It's a perfect morning for a hike." Owen was one of the student workers who were assigned to the camp for summer.

"Dangerous." Raphael 's face was impassive.

"Why?" Ken, a hefty Nisei high school football player from Oyama asked.

"Ravens." Raphael's face was deadpan. "Raven will fly down and steal your eyes."

A few of them looked at him quizzically while others kicked their boots and tried not to laugh. This was Raphael's territory, so nobody wanted to contradict him. Raphael polished a truck mirror that was already clean as he told his story. "The first crew that came through here didn't ask permission and things finished up very badly for them."

"The mosquitoes probably carried them away." Larry's high voice piped in. He was a first-year university hot shot from Vancouver who always made a joke of things, but he could sing like a choirboy.

"There was a massacre," Raphael stated in a flat voice.

Whistle pinched the water hose closed and looked up worried. "Wow! Doesn't a massacre mean that someone got killed?" Whistle's real name was Vladimir, but everyone called him Whistle because he could imitate birdcalls with perfect trills and warbles. He had a face full of freckles and red blonde curly hair, and clung to his guitar with its soft chords and poetry that he sang when he was alone. The crew teased him because he didn't know the same songs as them. "Everyone knows Winchester Cathedral," Larry insisted. "Listen!" He sounded out a whistled version of his own, but Whistle refused to repeat it. The more they teased him the more he tuned them out, so they learned not to push him too hard. He tried to be like one of the guys, but it didn't often work. He was friendly and genuine but he was tongue-tied when it came to expressing ideas about politics, culture, or the music of the day.

Raphael stroked his bronzed hairless chin and said, "Sometimes their spirits speak to me." Everyone looked up at the cliffs as if wailing ghosts would float out of the caves. Whistle was as transfixed as the rest of them but when the others looked back at Raphael for more of the story, they saw his hand do an underhand flip that lobbed a pebble into Whistle's open mouth. His aim was perfect. Whistle never saw the stone coming. When it landed on his tongue, he bent double in a fit of spitting and coughing like he had swallowed a fly. If Raphael tricked a person more than once it was a sign of inattention, but this was Whistle's third time.

When the laughter had died down and everyone was done poking and shoving each other, Raphael picked up his story. "A hundred years ago some bad things happened around here. Our guys were holed up in those caves because they killed some white guys in a fight about food so their families didn't starve. When the government tricked them into coming down for peace talks, they arrested all the chiefs and strung them up for murder."

The city boys had yet to tame a forest fire, much less imagine a public hanging. They had been hired as a first response mobile fire crew, thrown together by accident to replace some of the native workers who had previously been employed in fire control. When it was discovered that some of the local men were setting the fires themselves to earn extra money, the government hired university students to replace them, except for the trusted Raphael.

"People don't like the idea of you government guys going up there." Raphael was silent for a moment before he turned and walked away, clearly in a sudden bad mood. As he left he tossed his washrag into a bucket with such force that dirty water splashed up onto the fender of the clean truck.

At the beginning of the season there was occasional rain and on those days, 'Ranger Rod', a permanent Forest Service employee who lived in Alexis Creek, showed up in camp to conduct training sessions with pumps and shovels. With his perfectly pressed and accessorized khaki uniform and sandy crew cut, topped with a non-regulation Smokey the Bear campaign hat, he was the type of government bench-warmer who was attempting to work his way up to a forest district manager's job in the city. If his uniform got a smudge of dirt, he set to brushing it and slapping it like it was on fire. They called him Hot Rod behind his back because he thought he was one. When he stopped by camp for a visit, his sidekick

Travis accompanied him, though Rod always insisted on driving. Travis was only a few years older than the crew and had a knack of getting in the way of his superior's demonstrations, so he was instructed to stay on the sidelines unless he was summoned. Raphael, who didn't need any training, entertained himself by twirling his lariat, and when Hot Rod wasn't looking, laying a rope circle on the ground that Travis unwittingly walked into. The rope was yanked tight around his unsuspecting ankles and Travis fell over in the dust like a toppling telephone pole. Raphael smiled his Buddha smile, shrugged his shoulders, and waited for the victim to free himself.

Larry had been one of the first arrivals and had sized up Travis with the intention of asking him to buy a case of beer for the crew and keeping quiet about it. None of the crew were old enough to drink legally and bringing alcohol into camp was forbidden, so Larry and Ken, who's real name was Kenji, intended to get around the prohibition by ordering out.

On a Friday evening Larry's cabin mate Owen was designated to ask the camp foreman Bob for permission to take one of the trucks into Alexis Creek to mail a letter. There were rumours that Bob and his wife Marie were partial to vodka so if the beer purchase ever came to light, they figured that Bob couldn't be too harsh on them. The letter-mailing story was hardly convincing, but Bob had sympathy with the young crew's need to get out, so with a stern word about government property, he handed over the keys.

The village of Alexis Creek was like a hiccup in the scratch of unpaved highway that ran from the Fraser River plateau to the Pacific Ocean. The town's location had no particular geographic features, as if someone had picked it out on paper with a mapping pin. On the high side of the highway that traversed the gentle slope, was the two-story cinder block hotel with its moneymaking bar underneath. The Post Office across the street was a rough plank storefront with a wide shaded veranda that resembled an old west saloon with its walls decorated in the fluttering shreds of outdated announcements. A few steps East along the road was the prewar shiplap general store that sold rope, mosquito repellent and tinned vegetables. Opposite, a mechanic's shop surrounded by wrecked cars with all of the hoods lifted, marked the end of town. The bar in the hotel was off limits to the young men but they were told it was a wild place where fights broke out most weekends. Beer, blood and jealousy spilled into the parking lot between the hotel and the general store.

This parking lot was where the beer exchange took place. As arranged, Travis sauntered over to the double cab forestry truck with a case of cold beer under his arm. He greeted the crew in the truck as if their meeting had been a coincidence and when Larry the money collector handed over the funds, the case of beer slid through the passenger window and disappeared under a canvas jacket on the floor. Travis walked away with a discrete profit in hand and the truck drove off in the opposite direction from camp.

Ten miles up Pelican Lake Road they found a side track that opened into a clearing where they turned the truck around in case they had to make a quick exit.

"Hot Rod might have sent spies after us," Larry put on his cool city sunglasses. "It's all a set-up with Travis to get us all fired."

"You're paranoid," Owen said. "He has other things on his mind." Owen rolled down his side window now that they were stopped and the dust had settled. "Marie told me when I was on KP, that Rod's worried about what his wife gets up to when he's not home." There were crude remarks and raucous laughter that rolled around the clearing and dissipated in the dense and dusty pine forest.

Since there were four thirsty mouths in the truck and twelve bottles of beer, it was agreed that three each was enough to get drunk but show up in camp still able to walk. Larry, Ken and Owen, the ringleaders talked like they were old hands at drinking though it was doubtful any of them had consumed more than a couple of beers at family barbecues. Larry boasted about crossing the US border to go drinking because the age down there was only eighteen. There was more shouting and ribbing when it was apparent that nobody had brought a bottle opener.

"Wait, wait," Ken held up his hands. "Give me one of those bottles!" Whistle handed him a bottle from the cardboard carton. Ken reached into his pocket and pulled out a lighter.

"A firebug!" Owen called out and punched Ken's shoulder.

"Are you going to heat it up until the top pops off?" Whistle tried to demonstrate his home-schooled knowledge of physics but got only rolled eyes instead.

"Watch and learn." Kenji held the base of the bottle between his knees and made a fist below the neck. He caught the end of the lighter under an edge of the cap and with a sharp twist of his hand, the cap pinged and flipped over to the driver's lap. Ken had taught himself how to do a few tricks to make himself accepted and popular, less foreign than his Oriental features. He was an only son, so his parents expected him to take over the family orchard they had grown from seedlings when they were released from the Kootenay internment camp after the war. Though their Kenji was only just out of high school, he was an imposing young man, built like a Sumo wrestler, probably twice the size of his parents. At home he was in full rebellion mode, constantly swearing and telling everyone that he wasn't interested in "fuckin' apples". He intended to go to University and party.

By the end of the second beer the group were light-headed and flying high. Larry had started singing "The Sloop John B", an entry point to his repertoire of musical bookmarks. On the long truck rides to and from distant fires, mountain lookouts or special projects like restocking the ranger's cabin, Larry usually managed to convince the others to sing along with him. He assigned parts and tried to teach harmony, knocked out beats on the dashboard and directed the singers with an expressive hand. Larry was a lanky city boy with a blonde coif and a hawk nose that kept him on the downside of pretty. As much as he pushed his colleagues to make music with him, he was too ambitious and lost most of them by the second verse of his nasal Desolation Row.

Between bouts of laughter, shouts and singing, the young men took turns stumbling to the edge of the clearing to piss away the accumulated beer. During the third and final bottle Larry suggested they play true confessions, to admit to something they had never told anyone.

"You start," Ken raised his beer to Larry

"Okay." Larry was ready to play. "You know those ceiling sprinklers in school hallways? I was running down the hall one day and started jumping up to see if I could touch them. When I actually hit one it surprised me but even worse I accidentally knocked the head off. The entire school sprinkler system started off and did about $50,000 worth of damage. I never told anyone. They thought it was a faulty sprinkler that popped off on its own."

"Okay," Ken said. "Try this for size. Do you guys know what happens when you mix sodium and water?"

"Salt." Whistle remembered something from chemistry lessons.

"No man," Ken said. "You're such a wimp." He took a sip on his beer to cover the fact that nobody took up his jibe at Whistle. "Sodium," he said. "I'm talking sodium metal. I found some in the lab and put a big honking chunk of it down the toilet. You should have seen what happened. Blew the bowl right off the fucking floor. Fan-fuckin'-tastic!"

When the others turned to Whistle for his confession, he froze like a pit-lamped deer.

"You must have something," Larry said. "Never even picked your nose and eaten it."

"I....ah...yesterday."

"Aw Jeez," Larry said. "We don't want to know the details. "That's all you've got?" There was a look of panic on Whistle's face.

"Some boys peed on me," he said and looked down at the beer bottle in his hands.

"Why the hell did you let them do that?" Larry turned forward in his seat and glanced over at Ken.

"They were older." Whistle said. "They pushed me. I wasn't allowed to tell."

"Jeez, that's awful," Ken said , but Owen heard sarcasm and saw that the two in the front seat were trading punches with each other.

"I had to stay out of the house till my clothes dried."

"I've got something," Owen said in a sacrifice move to take the heat off Whistle. In fact, Owen didn't have anything in particular in mind, but the beer swimming in his head made him throw caution to the wind. He was often the mediator of the group, halfway between the stubborn rebelliousness of youth and the unwelcome reality of the adult world. Physically he was also medium, medium height, medium brown hair, not bad looking but not a model. "I'm still a virgin," he said quickly and quietly, half hoping it might be missed, knowing there was a high risk of ridicule.

"Come on! Get off it." Larry spoke for the group and lunged toward the back seat to grab at Owen. "None of them hot honey ever jumped your bones?"

"Not so far," Owen said, sure that there were a few other virgins present in the truck. They messed up his hair, tried to grab between his legs, and Ken made faces like he wanted to kiss him.

Whistle had sunk in his corner of the seat, sipping on his beer like it was a baby bottle that never strayed far from his lips.

"Wouldn't it be a blast," Larry said, "if we had a trial, a kangaroo court with you as the freshly deflowered virgin. We could haul some poor bugger up for getting you pregnant."

"That new guy with the glasses...what's his name." Ken frowned.

"Teddy. Yeah, he'd be a good one." Larry said. "We can kidnap him and say he took advantage of a poor young innocent thing like you. He won't know what the hell happened." There was a chorus of lewd suggestions and laughter. Larry started singing "Wild Thing" and Whistle spilled beer on his shirt.

Owen and Teddy had gone to High School at the same time but had never spoken to each other. With buck teeth, round wire framed glasses, and plastic pocket protector Teddy was labelled as a nerd, though his academic marks weren't all that good. However, in shop class it became apparent that his expertise was mechanical. His father had taught him how to strip down a Land Rover and put it back together; a skill that eventually silenced those who called him a nerd.

"We could set up our courtroom down at the end of the camp where the trees start." Larry was in theatre mode.

"Can we have a fire?" Whistle came to life. "I know we put them out and all, but we haven't had you know, a fire. I can bring my guitar...."

"Bob will probably let us burn some of the lumber from that shed we tore down." Owen suggested. "We could make like we're doing a favour."

"Let's do it," Larry jumped around in his seat, charged up to be organizing something. "But for fuck's sake, don't let any of this get back to Teddy."

On the way back to camp Whistle threw up on the floor of the back seat. It was the first vehicle that Bob inspected in the morning and there was still a stink of stale beer and vomit. A lecture on trust and responsibility followed. The four offenders were ordered to wash all the trucks inside and out before lunch and were further confined to camp for a week except for fire calls. Bob the foreman promised them that if Ranger Rod ever got wind of the incident he would send the culprits one by one to a furthest fire lookout where they could each spend a few weeks on their own with black cloud hail storms and ear splitting lightning for company.

Their punishment fuelled the plan to hold a trial. After a few days of sticking close to base, Owen suggested to the foreman that they would like to relieve their boredom by having a fire one evening to burn the remains of the tar paper and sawdust shack they had torn down to make room for a tent floor. There would be no alcohol of course, and at dusk when the fire was already a good size, Bob limped down to make sure of that.

Whistle strummed on his guitar though he had to stay back from the fire as the acrid smoke from burning tar made him cough. Teddy was present at the bonfire along with the rest of the crew, not all of whom knew about the plan. Any other adult supervision like Raphael had gone home for the night. Bob was satisfied and limped back to the cook-shack.

"Probably off to drink vodka and fuck his wife," Ken said. "Lucky bugger."

"Her? Come on! She must be at least forty."

"Old enough to know what she wants," Ken said. "I'm sure I caught her checking me out."

By the time it was truly dark and the fire had consumed the flammable chaff and settled down to burning timber, a few of the more responsible crew drifted back to their shacks from boredom. Teddy was on the verge of following them when Larry called over to him from the other side of the fire. "Hey buddy! I saw you with a big fancy flashlight the other day. That would be handy out here. How 'bout you go get it?"

"Mmm..." Teddy was reluctant. "I don't really want to lend it out. It's one of my tools."

"Teddy it's important." Larry looked over his shoulder toward the flickering shadowed woods. "We can hear things out there, and with your light we can spot any beasties that come around."

Everyone including Teddy peered into the gloom and tall fir trees that hemmed in the clearing on three sides.

"I saw an owl swoop jump down from the trees and fly right toward the fire," Whistle said.

The others looked at him doubtfully because nobody else had seen it. "Must have disappeared in the grass," he offered, to explain its absence.

"Owls don't jump," Owen said. "They fly. They hop off their perch and glide." He made movement with one hand like an airplane coming in to land.

Ted looked back to Ken. An invisible owl didn't require his flashlight.

"Wolves," Ken said, squinting at the dark forest. "This is their territory."

Teddy didn't know enough about wolves to contradict him. "Okay," he said, though he sounded doubtful. "I'll be back in five minutes."

When Teddy had almost reached the camp, Larry sent Ken and a few henchmen trotting after him.

"Bring back a couple of chairs!" he shouted after them.

While the group was away fetching Teddy, Owen changed into his role by shoving a couple of oranges into the pockets of his khaki work shirt, tying the arms of a jacket around his waist for a skirt, and making a kerchief out of red bandanna he had borrowed from Whistle for the occasion.

When the group came back with Teddy, his hands were tied behind his back and there was a gag over his mouth. He was struggling and his eyes that were wider and bluer than usual, flashed between laughter, surprise, and anger. His escort sat him down roughly on a chair at one side of the campfire and tied his legs to the rungs. Out of the dark, Owen appeared with his headscarf and bunched up jacket in the front to indicate pregnancy.

"Sit," Larry commanded and pushed Owen down into a chair opposite Teddy. Larry had pulled a pair of white briefs over his hair to resemble a judicial wig.

"Judge Larry Knightshadez The Third presiding."

Laughter.

"Silence!" he ordered. "Sergeant. Remove the muzzle from the mouth of the accused. Let us hear what the accused has to say for himself."

"What the fuck's going on?" Teddy spat out when he was able to talk. He looked around for some other help besides the judge but nobody spoke up.

With his underpants wig and inside out jacket worn over his shoulders for a cape, Larry strode back and forth in front of the jury. "It should be clear," he said, turning his attention to Owen, the wronged party. "That this unfortunate woman, an innocent virgin once destined to be the loving wife of an unfaithful husband, has now been ruined by your unbridled lust and complete. You have shown a complete disregard for the position of this poor creature."

Teddy opened his mouth as if to defend himself but no words came out. There was silence, the fire crackled and a hoot from the bush that really did sound like an owl.

"She told me that she wanted it Sir," he tilted his chin toward the judge. Teddy had decided to play along.

"Well?" The judge towered over the supposed victim.

"I don't know about these things Sir." Owen muttered to his lap. "He gave me this." He fished a condom out of a shirt pocket and held it up to the judge. "He said I would like it."

"Give me that thing," Larry snatched the condom out of Owen's hand, unrolling it as he strode across to Teddy's chair. He held the full length of rubber up against Teddy's face. "You know what this is?"

"Yes Sir."

"Is it yours?"

"No Sir."

There were jeers from the crowd and Whistle in his excitement to get a better look at what was being held up as evidence, tripped on a board sticking out of the fire, and was only saved from landing face first in the flames by Ken who noticed and shoved him aside. Whistle looked offended when he stood up and brushed himself.

"Silence!" Larry the judge called out. "If you're not careful you'll be next on the stand."

Whistle did his best to disappear into the background behind the spectators, though he couldn't see anything from there.

"You perjure yourself my friend," Larry flipped his cape in flamboyant imitation of a grandstanding prosecutor. "The victim happens to be a special personal friend of mine, aren't you sweetie." He sidled up to the pregnant victim.

Owen batted his eyelashes at the judge and there were catcalls from the gallery. "Silence!" Larry shouted. He pointed to Owen. "She wouldn't lie, would you honey."

"I'm innocent. The jury has been rigged." Ted protested, though he was more laughing than taking the verdict seriously.

"Guilty! Guilty as charged!" Larry shouted. "Take him away!" He pointed back to the camp. Someone behind the small group clapped his hands, which made Larry turn back and narrow his eyes at them.

Ted made a serious attempt to run for it once he was on foot, but faster feet caught up and wrestled him to the ground. Owen laughed so much that when he was untangling himself from his skirts, he pissed himself. Whistle was still there, and they could see the guys dragging Ted toward one of the cabins. To keep his accident secret, Owen told Whistle, "Go. Go after them." Whistle was reluctant but eventually walked away with his guitar, his head down like he was being sent for his own punishment. He looked back a few times toward the fire to see if Owen was following but Owen pretended to be busy and gestured for Whistle to go on ahead. Owen hadn't admitted when it was confession time, that pissing himself when laughing was a humiliating weakness that had plagued him since childhood.

In the dark he detoured to his own cabin to change his trousers. Because Teddy stayed in the cabin next door he could hear banging and shouting but he was in too much of a hurry to pull off his boots and stash his wet jeans to think about what was happening to Teddy.

He heard afterward that they stripped him naked and threw cold water on him. He had defended himself valiantly but the conspirator on guard saw the foreman's light go on and the group had to abandon their punishment and sneak round the back way to their cabins. The foreman didn't check on them that night but asked about the commotion the next day. Teddy said that he had tripped over something in the dark, fell down and set off a chain reaction that woke everyone up. His collusion cemented his inclusion in the group, and he laughed along with the rest of them when they talked about what they had done to him. Being part of an inner circle was something that didn't often happen to Teddy. His opinion now had more weight, especially in the field of mechanics where he was listened to and respected.

In July, Whistle got a letter from a friend inviting him to come to Vancouver to live in a commune and share his music with them. Some of the original crew found other jobs in the city and replacements arrived for them, though most didn't last long, turning up their city noses at the dirty work of digging fire guards and living in relatively primitive conditions. When out on fires they didn't bother with tents but slept rolled up in sleeping bags. The veterans knew it was better to sleep with their boots stuffed into their down sleeping bag to avoid having them drenched with dew in the morning. Back at camp they had roofs over their heads but every morning someone in each cabin had to get up to light the wood fire so the others could get dressed in some comfort. Running water was available in the cold washhouse down in the ravine behind camp.

A few of the original crew were still in residence at the beginning of September, just before the university semester sent them back to school. One evening after Ken had finished his KP of dinner dishes, he stopped by Larry and Owen's cabin to tell them what he had heard from Marie the cook.

"She read in The Province that the guy we called Whistle, Vladimir, he died in an accident in Vancouver. There was a demonstration outside a Catholic Church downtown about finding the graves of Residential School children, and I guess Whistle sneaked in the door. They found him on the grass under the tallest bell tower. They think he fell."

"Dumb kid," Owen said, but wondered if Whistle's death was an accident or not.

"Freaky," Larry said. "Freaky deaky." Whistle was the first person any of them had known who was dead.

Owen imagined Whistle looking down at his beat up city shoes as he teeters on the parapet that surrounds the cathedral's tallest gothic tower. He looks up, bends his knees slightly, gives a push and falls forward, diving like a moonlit owl, until he makes an almost silent thud on the small patch of grass below the steeple.

The young men are certain that the tragic death had nothing to do with them.

Antipodes

If she had taken the half hour orbital flight instead of the cheaper four-hour sonic ticket to get to the other side of the world, the arrival procedures would have been the same. People weren't used to sitting still for so long and once moving, they were in a rush to go on their way, but informed travellers knew that before the plane doors opened a disinfecting mist would be pumped into the cabin. A few claustrophobic passengers, more exasperated by the delay than the spray, couldn't keep their expletives to themselves. The odd returning citizen spoke up to defend his country's reasoning, but it did little to quell the general muttering. Everyone wanted out.

"Wait until they get chipped," said an older, locally accented woman who sat with Juliette on the flight and was now behind her as they waited in another airlock between exits. "They'll make you swallow a six month one even if you're here only for a week . Most everyone has a permanent one now." Juliette didn't know if the woman meant this was good or bad, though there was a bit of a sigh after she spoke. "Better just to take your medicine." She smiled sweetly and pretended to be interested in the other passengers.

Juliette had come to see her old friend Carol. They had lived in a cooperative housing project in Vancouver ten years earlier that had disbanded when jealousy and bickering overtook the residents' need for communal housing. The occupants had flown like fledgling birds toward whatever youthful enthusiasms appeared on their radar, which for Carol meant travelling to Peru to study natural dyes and textiles. Within a year she had a child with a German Peruvian man who worked at the storefront of his mother's weaving cooperative. When news came that anti-government gangs had carried out a series of murders and kidnappings, she began to worry about her son's safety, and after victims were picked off in the next village, she had followed a friend, another foreign mother like her, home to Boracamba on the empty continent to restart her life somewhere safe. The boy's father ran the other direction, back to the safety of his father's family in Germany.

When Carol arrived down under, she first found work selling frozen fish to farmers from a camper van, and later switched to a used furniture venture with a new boyfriend. Juliette was of the opinion that it would have been easier for Carol to return to Canada with her son instead of running off to the other side of the world, but Carol always did things her way, demonstrating a rebellious streak that had pulled her away from the family farm as soon as she finished school.

Juliette was an independent person as well, an only child who had made her own share of questionable choices. Her most recent mistake had lasted five years and had come to an abrupt halt when her boyfriend punched her in the stomach during an argument about his infidelity. From the beginning she knew he had violence in him but thought she had tamed the beast. It was a shame the story was over, but she was relieved all the same because when she was with him her life was more war than peace.

When the boyfriend was gone, the rent on the house they shared was too expensive, so before she moved to a single condo, she called her friend Carol.

"Don't you ever think about coming back to Canada?"

"I'm as good as settled in here." Carol was positive and upbeat. "Sorry to hear about your break-up though. Why don't you fly down and stay with us for a while?" she suggested.

Juliette took a month off work for the trip, stored what sticks of furniture she had acquired, gave her plants away, keeping in mind that she might change her life completely and stay with Carol for good. Circumstances would make the decision clear. She didn't confirm with Carol that she was coming as she planned to arrive unannounced at her door.

When the auto-cab left the airport for Carol's house, a band of rain swept over the highway, pelting down hard enough that Juliette had misgivings about her safety as the driverless car sped blithely through the curtain of water. She had expected to land in a sunny country, and sure enough by the time they arrived in Carol's Swanbourne neighbourhood, the blinding sun had already dried the exposed pavement. Overcome by a wave of jetlag, she asked the car to open a roof vent and was wrapped in the exotic scent of jasmine, of heady frangipani, and the whiff of ocean ozone that coiled through the balmy air. The rows of spiky palms that slid by the windows, the gangling Norfolk pines, and papery eucalyptus, were alien to her northern eye. When she spotted a flock of parrots hopping from one magnolia tree to another, she sat up amazed, thrilled to have arrived somewhere so strange.

Up on the front porch, Carol's head poked out the front door so Juliette waved the auto-cab away. Carol's mouth dropped open and as she stepped barefoot onto the porch, she let out an excited scream and reached up to wrap her arms around Juliette's neck. Carol was much the same as the last time they'd met, slim and petite with short dark hair that she kept in a boyish cut. She often stood with one shoulder lower than the other, a posture that people mistakenly took for deference, but Juliette had seen her fire off some zinging one-liners from that go-for-your-gun position. She had a laugh like the rise and fall of tinkling glasses in a wine bar. Juliette, the taller of the two, in her usual jeans and a plaid shirt, straight auburn hair kept long, high cheekbones and sun freckles across her nose, looked more like an Alberta cowgirl than Carol who was born to it. Carol had made some sexual advances when they first met and after agreeing that they were attracted to each other, they both admitted that they preferred male partners.

Carol's boyfriend Gregg came to the door and was sent out immediately to buy a box of wine. Carol called for her son Thomas who had stayed in his room to avoid the adult commotion, to come and meet her friend. Thomas was ten years old, with reddish hair and olive skin. He wore belted shorts pulled up too high for his waist and a dark blue long sleeve shirt that was buttoned up to the neck. Carol was casual about how she dressed, favouring tailored shorts and light airy tunics topped with woven textile waistcoats she had made herself. Juliette smiled to see that Thomas might take after his more rigid absent father. The boy studied Juliette with a serious expression while his mother explained who she was. "We were best friends before you were born," she said.

"I need a snack mum," he said, unimpressed with the visitor.

As Carol assembled his hundreds-and-thousands sandwich she explained her domestic situation to Juliette. "Greg doesn't live here even though we're officially husband and wife. We got married so Thomas and I could get citizenship. We lived together for about a year until our papers came through and then Gregg moved into a place of his own. He comes round to do some gardening for me and takes Thomas out for guy activities."

"I never understood why you came here instead of Canada," Juliette asked. Thomas looked at his mother as well, waiting for her answer.

"It's complicated," she said and sent Thomas into the back garden with his sandwich, so the sprinkles didn't scatter all over the kitchen floor. She motioned Juliette to sit down at the table that straddled the kitchen and what Carol called the lounge, though every time she said the word, Juliette had to resist looking around for cocktail menus.

"Gregg will be gone for a while," Carol said. "They only have the wine he likes up at the bottle shop in Subiaco. If we knew you were coming, we would have stocked up."

Juliette was in no hurry. Her jetlag didn't dictate a need to drink, but Carol seemed to think it was required.

"What kind of work does he do?" she asked, looking at the lounge walls that were hung with Carol's weaving projects, nothing to indicate any influence from Gregg.

"Oh, he doesn't work," Carol said.

"So, what does he do?"

"Nothing really. Hangs out with his mechanic mates and football buddies. His pension pays enough that he doesn't need to work."

"He doesn't look old enough for a pension." Her first impression had pegged him at about forty.

"It's a disability pension. He had some problems with the law when he was younger, and the government figures it's cheaper to keep people like him on the outside instead of paying to keep him in jail. He gets paid enough to keep him from going back to his old ways. He was trying to feed a drug problem back then, so he got involved in some shady money-making scams."

"You mean he gets paid by the government not to steal?"

Carol got up from the table, perhaps offended by Juliette's incredulous tone and put away the sandwich makings while she talked. "It's part of the subsidy system they put in a few years ago. Everyone gets a basic income."

"Then why would anyone want to work?"

"People can work to earn more on top of the subsidy if they want. I could stop work if I like but I need the extra money."

The front screen door slammed behind Gregg and he plonked a two-litre box of Chardonnay down on the table. "I thought we'd have a proper knees-up in honour of your visit. Straight from God's own country down in Adeline River," he drawled as he popped the spigot at the bottom of the box while Carol fetched three unbreakable plastic tumblers.

"Knock 'em back girlies." Gregg raised his full glass to the company.

During the next few weeks as Juliette accompanied Carol on errands, she saw that the city had a downtown core of a few blocks and outlying neighbourhood hubs, but most of it was an urban sprawl of single-family dwellings. "Owning a piece of land is every man's dream," Carol said. The suburbs radiated from the city centre until they tapered off to endless eucalyptus patches. Some of the most desirable residences were concentrated into California bungalows near the beaches on the Indian Ocean.

Because Carol's father had recently sold the family ranch in Alberta and split the proceeds with his daughters, Carol had been able to buy a house of her own. Her son was ready to start school, so she had chosen Swanbourne, halfway between the city centre and the beach, because it was a quiet leafy neighbourhood to grow up in. She was proud of her hundred-year-old house with its red Jarrah wood floors, sleek corrugated steel roofing, and a pierced building-block garden wall that offered privacy from the street. Behind the house was a covered patio to accommodate the essential barbecue and at the end of the garden was a seldom used dunny with a posted warning about Redback spiders.

Juliette found it difficult to warm to Gregg though he wasn't a bad person. In local jargon he was an "ocker", a redneck with racist views that Juliette, a diehard socialist, couldn't help calling him out on. She soon learned that it was better to let some of his remarks go unopposed because their disagreements were so frequent that Carol often had to step into the awkward position of peacemaker. Gregg, with his beer belly and thinning hair, was old enough to be Thomas's grandfather but Carol thought he was a good male presence for the boy, one that would toughen him up for the society he would face in the future. Juliette couldn't imagine what reactionary ideas he put into the boy's head, but at least he was wise enough not to pretend to be Thomas's father. Thomas told his mates at school that his real father was an astronaut.

On a clear blue sky Sunday, when a lavender haze of jacarandas blossoms lay over the city, Gregg took Thomas to a football game at the Leederville Oval, so Carol and Juliette took a car down to the dunes along Marine Parade to spend the afternoon at the beach. Juliette was determined to fish a straight answer out of Carol about why she was living so far away. It was true the weather was better, and Juliette did like the place, comparing it to a cross between England and California, but she suspected there were other reasons Carol had decided to stay.

"You've got to admit that it's not a bad life," Carol said as they shook out beach towels under their umbrella.

"It seems easy enough, but I can't help thinking that it's too easy, too comfortable. You've got everything laid on for you. Don't you worry when the government pays for everything, that they want to control everything? What happens if you don't behave the way you're supposed to?"

"They can do things to you." Carol admitted. "Like limit your travel options, or deduct money from your subsidy, or even take your pets away. But why would you want to do something bad? It's like public video cameras or microchips. If you're not doing anything illegal why would you worry about them."

"I don't know. The idea of being watched all of the time gives me the creeps. I can't wait until this chip they gave me expires, if it ever does."

Carol had positioned their umbrella so that the two of them were facing the sea with nothing in front of them except sandy beach and turquoise water.

"Don't fool yourself that you're not watched when you're back home in Canada," Carol said.

Juliette craned her neck to look behind their umbrella but could only see empty dunes with patches of sea tolerant Darwinia. "Maybe I should be nervous just talking to you," she said.

Carol laughed. "People here have this outlaw streak. They know how to get around things if they want to. That's part of what made up my mind to stay. It's what I want for Thomas." She pushed her heels into the sand in front of her to make a cool groove for her calves then dug her hands into the sand at her sides until they disappeared. She looked from one buried hand to the other as if wondering where they had gone then pulled them out and brushed off the white sand, which sprinkled her tanned legs.

"I've never believed in what's good for one is good for all", Carol said, and shook her short hair in the onshore sea breeze. "Thomas was born in Peru so we couldn't get all of those fancy medical checks and vaccinations. I wouldn't have dreamed about giving him a flu vaccine when he was six months old even if I could have. I lied at immigration and told them that Peru didn't have the latest vaccine technology so we would get them done here."

"Did you?" Juliette asked.

Carol shook her head but didn't look at her friend. It was her way of avoiding conflict. Something in her past, made her avoid eye contact when she thought she might be challenged. Juliette had seen her talk over people's shoulders instead of to their faces.

"Has he had the basic shots?" Juliette asked. "You don't want to be playing roulette with him."

"No," Carol said as if she was casually turning down an offer to contribute to a charity.

When Juliette didn't react, Carol took the time to explain. "You probably had the measles," she said. "And chicken pox and mumps, and for sure we have both had the flu and a few worse things besides, but I believe that most of these vaccinations are forced on us. Some people think that having measles when you're small gives you better protection from heart diseases when you're older, stuff like that. These days polio and smallpox have been almost eliminated so why get jabs for non-existent diseases?"

"But it's not fair if your child is protected by the other kids who are doing what they are supposed to."

"Okay," Carol said. "Guilty as charged, but I don't think he's going to catch anything nasty. He's a young boy and he's healthy so he has natural immunity."

"But things like measles and mumps can be deadly."

"Measles didn't suddenly get more deadly than when we had them. The flu can be deadly, and a cold can turn into pneumonia. We can't protect everyone from everything. It's not natural. When Thomas was a baby, I practically encouraged him to eat dirt. I kept him clean, but I wasn't running around wiping his hands and face every two seconds. If he picked up something and put it in his mouth it didn't bother me...as long as it wasn't poisonous or dog shit. Kids get immunity from exposure."

"How can he go to school if he isn't vaccinated?"

"The health department calls him compromised. But a lot of old folks or people with chronic health problems are labelled compromised. It's a big category so he's not alone. I pay for a private school because they're more open-minded and discrete about these things. The government knows what he's had and what he hasn't, and they deduct money from my subsidy to punish me for his missing shots."

Juliette studied the long lines of waves that broke diagonally along the beach, and it reminded her that she must check to see if the water here drained out of the sink in the opposite direction than it did at home. A few times since she had been there she thought about where she was positioned on the globe, and sometimes it felt like she was upside down, and now she felt a bit dizzy listening to the incorrect logic of her friend. "So why didn't you go back to Canada when you had to leave Peru?" she asked. "You could have figured out something back home."

"Well, apart from this," Carol opened her arms toward the beach and the turquoise sea, "Canada is a lot stricter and law abiding. Here people are less likely to rat you out if you're up to something you're not supposed to be. The heroes here are people who give the finger to the law and get away with it. And I've always been a black sheep as you know." Juliette was surprised when Carol leaned over and kissed her on the cheek.

Juliette sighed. Her friend was right. Carol had usually done what she wanted against everyone's advice but had always landed on her feet. "Okay, you stubborn old boot," Juliette laughed. "Have it your way. Let's have a sip of that wine you brought, unless drinking on the beach is against the law too."

"Oh, it's illegal all right, but there aren't any coppers around that I can see. We can knock it back all day and nobody gives a toss if you keep your eyes peeled for the patrol and aren't too obvious."

Juliette sipped from her glass and mulled over her friend's choices. She wouldn't have taken the same road but criticizing her friend for going her own way was pointless. Everyone has their own logic and does what they think is best for them. Juliette had to admit that even she wasn't convinced that societies should control individuals too closely, from every bite they ate, to what their thoughts should be. Carol believed she was living life by her own lights, though it looked to Juliette like she had surrendered one kind of control for another.

In a place that looked so much like paradise, a continent sized island with a willing population, a kind climate, in a country where flocks of pink galahs bicker overhead and scarlet flame trees line residential streets, it was easy to shrug one's shoulders when asked about what the state was doing to maintain balance in such a perfect world. Like people, states do what they think they need to do.

Carol raised her glass. "A wise man changes himself to fit the world," she said. "And a fool tries to change the world to fit himself. That means progress depends on fools like me." Carol had learned to take difficulties in stride from her father on the farm, though in the end he had given up his dream because his girls weren't interested in an agricultural future.

When they got home from the beach Gregg was there by himself pacing between the lounge and kitchen.

"Where's Thomas?" Carol looked inquisitively toward her son's room.

"I would have called you if I could." Gregg was flushed and out of breath. One of the conditions of his pension was that he couldn't own portable media.

"Where is Thomas?" Carol was suddenly alarmed.

"I don't know," Gregg looked down ashamed. "We were on the way home from the game and he wanted to show me how smart he was. Right before the station we split up to go around the block our separate ways and meet up at the end."

He looked up at Carol, partly fearful and partly defiant. His eyes were wide and bulging. "He wasn't there. He never showed up. I went round and round everywhere calling for him and I never found him. I waited at the station, but he never showed."

Carol was dumbstruck. "Did you call the police when you got home?"

"Not yet."

"Fuck. I don't believe it." Carol paced around the kitchen like a caged animal, making phone calls to police, fire, and ambulance, anyone she could think of who looked for missing children, and firing all kinds of insults at Gregg that all boiled down to "How could you?"

The police showed up at the door early in the evening with an unfazed Thomas in tow. "I got to ride in an air cruiser mum!" If he had been afraid when he was lost, the process of being found and sent home had distracted him enough that he was happy to go to his room and play with his collection of toy dinosaurs like he did on most days.

The police questioned them on the details of the incident and when they scanned for microchips and saw that Carol didn't have one, they made her produce her documents of deferment. At the door on the way out they gave her a caution about her own status and a lecture about living with a known criminal, even if his nose was apparently clean.

It only took a day however, before a message arrived for Gregg with details about his reassignment to Boracamba, the small town in the dry wastelands of the interior where Carol had originally restarted her life with Thomas. When Gregg's name came up in the lost boy incident, the police had flagged his chip for a closer look and discovered that his acquaintances knew him as the bagman for a ring of false document suppliers. In cases like his, rather than spend the time and money for an investigation and arrest, the government's remedy was to separate him from his current life and to force him to start somewhere with less temptation. If he misbehaved again, they would move him to an even smaller town further into the outback. "Screw them," Gregg said. "I've moved too many times already. Makes me want to pull my chip and take off into the blue, maybe go back to the east coast and disappear into the city."

"Either way I'm not going with you," Carol told him. "It would mean selling the house, quitting my job and taking Thomas out of school." It was obvious that Gregg had served his purpose by sponsoring them for citizenship but if he couldn't keep his nose clean, that was not Carol's problem. "And we need to get a divorce," she added, "Before you disappear completely."

On a school morning a couple of days later, Thomas was late getting out of bed and when his mother checked on him, he claimed that he didn't feel like going to school. As she sat with him on the bed, asking what was wrong, she noticed a red line that had crept up the back of his calf. "What's this?" she traced the line with her finger, squinting at it to see if it was drawn with a red pen. He shrugged. "Did you step on something?" She poked various places on the bottom of his foot.

He frowned like it was something he would never do, but then his face cleared. "Oh yeah," he said. "When

Uncle Gregg lost me, I climbed through a fence and one of the boards must have had a nail because it stuck to my foot. I had my shoes on though."

At the hospital Carol threw herself across her son's body like an animal mother to prevent him getting a tetanus vaccine. She insisted it was redundant because their tests showed that he only had an infection, there was no sign of tetanus. The disapproving doctor gave her a prescription for antibiotics and sent her home with a threat about not helping people in future who wouldn't help themselves.

When Carol received her own unpleasant message with a bureaucratically worded threat to microchip, vaccinate or leave, she brushed it aside as another chess move in her battle to do what she thought was best for her son.

Even with renewed doubts about the legitimacy of her arranged marriage and her uncertain status as a citizen, Carol asked Juliette to stay on, to share the house and help with Thomas. But Juliette had already made up her mind. There was nothing to be gained from attaching herself to another family as a substitute aunt and sister. She needed to restart her own life. It was better to let Carol carry on with her logical or illogical choices on the flip side of the world.

When Juliette's month-long visit was up, Carol accompanied her to the airport. "Was it something I said?" she asked, only partly joking.

"No," Juliette had tried different ways to explain her decision to her friend. "Maybe it's the place," she said. "I'm used to where I live. It's beautiful here, but it's too exotic and strange for me. I feel disoriented, like things are turned on their head."

"You'd be a big help if you stayed." Carol made a last effort at the departure gate. "We could figure out a way to make it work."

"Call me," Juliette indicated as she wheeled her suitcase down the polished concourse wondering if her friend would ever call her, and if it would be an emergency request for asylum or a plea for help for Thomas.

Although living down under would be an adventure, Juliette was afraid of sinking into the addictive comfort of such a bird of paradise existence. The antipodean Eden had its bugs, cracks, and mutations that undermined its astonishing beauty. It was a place where criminals were set free and sickness was criminalized in an engineered experiment to create a perfect society, but with all of its technological wonders, Juliette didn't think anyone was better off. Certainly, the few aboriginals who remained were not. It was a better idea for her to start again in her home country, a place that had its own flaws, but the devils and diseases she would need to wrestle with would be ones she already knew.

Pillars Of Sand

"You cannot separate culture from language!" To put an end to the discussion John banged his empty glass on the sturdy taverna table, but when he let go of it, he hiccupped which knocked the tumbler over. Surprised by the mishap, he sat paralysed and detached, watching the glass roll to the point of no return, already curious about how and where the shards would scatter. One of his drinking companions, a fisherman, reached over and caught the glass in mid-flight and stood it upright on the table. The incident brought John around enough to refill it from the dregs in the bottle. The more he drank, the less he believed how much he had consumed. "It was just a couple of glasses," he'd protest, when everyone knew he had polished off two bottles of cheap white. "Mathematical propositions express no thoughts," he'd say and wave away the concept of counting drinks.

"We need to get him home," one of John's Greek friends muttered to an English painter at the table. John raised his full glass in the air to make a toast. "To life," he slurred. "We are asleep," he raised his voice and sat upright in his chair, " but we wake sometimes, sometimes..." He slumped back again, and his chin nodded toward his chest, though one hand still anchored to his glass like it was lashed to a mast in a pitching sea. Someone shook his shoulder. "Hey! Ela Yianni!" a voice said. "Time to go home."

John's head lifted but his eyes barely opened "... dreaming," he mumbled, finishing his thought before his chin hit his chest again. His companions nodded at each other; their friend was too far-gone to walk home. They'd need to commandeer the wheelbarrow that was kept outside the vegetable shop beside the taverna. Besides helping the short square wife of the greengrocer bring her produce to the shop, it doubled as a communal luggage carrier and was free to be pressed into service if it was returned intact. John was easier to control if he was a dead weight, knocked out by alcohol, because if he started flopping he would bail out of the barrow and stagger back to the taverna, bouncing off walls in the narrow streets, attempting to keep his spinning world on a vertical axis.

The village where John lived was a jumble of white cube houses that huddled behind a rocky headland whose high cliffs plummeted dizzyingly toward the sea. John's house was high up at the back of the village. There was a zigzag route without steps to get home from the taverna, but in the dark it was a complicated and strenuous climb. Some of the hills were so steep that even with two friends pushing, it took serious effort to gain enough momentum to transport their groaning cargo to the next level. The disadvantage of taking him home the long way round, was that they had to rush past the cemetery in the dark, a place where they had all witnessed relatives buried. Once past the spooky section with its black candle cypresses, the road to the top was easier. They could dump John off at the top of the cliff and he could find his way from there. It was only a few steps down to a steep trail that squeezed through a maze of vertical rock slabs that had broken off a quake-shattered necropolis. John sometimes woke up in this miniature canyon under a blaze of blue sky with no memory of why he had been cast into the biblical wilderness, only to realize that he was just a few steps from his front door.

"Peroni or Fix?" The taverna owner would ask when John stopped by for a beer in the afternoon.

"Knowledge is needed to make a choice," John said solemnly, "and I don't know what chance thing will influence my decision until the time comes."

"You're too smart for your own good Mister John." From habit the taverna keeper flattered his customers, and John was a good one. He winked so John knew he was playing with him. "But now that you are here," the man said, "the time has come. I will bring you a Fix."

John didn't get drunk every night but if he ran across the right people at the right time, he started and couldn't stop. Wheelbarrow John as his friends called him, laughed and joked when his friends suggested he drank too much, and he would paper it over with one of his philosophical nuggets, like "Nothing is so difficult as not deceiving oneself." He might swear off alcohol for a while and try to eat properly, but he'd never learned the mysteries of the kitchen, so if he drank a beer while figuring out what to eat, it would become a second beer and then he wasn't hungry anymore.

When he first arrived in the village, he was fluent in a strangely accented Greek because he had studied classical Greek at University. The locals tolerated him as an eccentric Hellenophile, but they didn't understand why he would give up a good life in America to live in their village.

"And where is his wife?" the local housewives would ask as they dried their hands on their aprons and tilted their noses toward his door, sure that he had a woman held prisoner in there. One of John's taverna buddies taught him how to spear grouper and octopus in exchange for reading and writing letters to his European girlfriends. "Say to her that my heart is big with love for her," the friend would dictate.

When it was too hot to write or study indoors, the balmy turquoise water that lapped at the base of the cliffs offered delicious relief on hot days as well as the possibility of catching supper. If he got lucky and caught a big enough fish, he offered the bounty to his friends hoping that one of them, or his wife, would cook dinner. Fishing was a way to focus his mind on something besides reading, writing, and the horrifying world news. He wasn't drawn to fishing for the joy of cavorting in the wonders of nature, but for the hunt. He and an American friend had a standing challenge and boasting rights about who could catch the biggest grouper. Like a gritty beachcomber who has no interest in the sky, John kept his head down and concentrated on winning the competition.

Most mornings he was to be found in Petros Bar with a metrio coffee, reading every article in the newest Herald Tribune. The cafe was the social hub, and since it was near the post office, his need for mail put him in treacherous proximity to the cafe's bar. "How about a coffee?" a friend would ask.

"With a splash of brandy thank you." John would beam whatever hospitable smile he could muster, something that depended on his condition the night before. If he was still at the cafe after midday, friends might arrive and order real drinks and maybe a meal. "Stay," they'd slap him on the back. "Where else are you going? You need to eat." John didn't like to spend his money on cafe food, but if there was a meal and serious conversation to be had, he stayed. "I'll just have a glass of wine," he'd say and signal to the cafe owner who would bring him a bottle. Later in the evening he would drink ouzo, which never failed to send him off to oblivion.

"Seriously John," a friend asked. "Why didn't you ever get married." John was almost fifty and so according to the rules of most cultures he should have long since settled down and had a family. He could have grandchildren by now.

"Once was enough," John wasn't comfortable talking about the past. He had been married but didn't consider it valid. "I'm not going to make that mistake again," was all he'd say.

He had been an assistant professor at Princeton when he met a California dream girl at a party. It was mutual infatuation, and they were desperate to live together, but their families were scandalized by their unconsecrated cohabitation. "Let's run away and get married," she said, so on a Spring Break they caught a Greyhound to Niagara Falls, said the words, and got the certificate. The honeymoon was short lived.

"I thought your father owned a department store," she said when he explained why they couldn't buy a second car.

"I told you he's the manager." He sat her down to explain why they couldn't have a bigger house and a fatherly allowance to pay for the trips and jewellery she expected. He was tied to the University, but she was interested in vacations with shopping trips. She wanted to spend every night out at the local clubs, but he had student's papers to grade.

"You're so old," she would say when he wouldn't go out dancing with her. "You're only twenty-four. We should be out having fun."

The more unsatisfied she was with her situation, the more she made embarrassing scenes at faculty gatherings. "I don't give a fuck what they think," she'd say as she tossed her clothes onto a chair in the bedroom after a night out. "How was I supposed to know that crude little weasel was the president of the University?"

In their second winter together, she left him to go back to California. He didn't hear from her until the divorce papers arrived in the mail. "It's better that way," he told his parents, who didn't need convincing. Once he had signed the papers and sent them off, his heart squeezed tight under the weight of sadness for lost adventures, unborn children, and a tender old age together that would never be. Maybe later someone would come along to be his companion for life but while he waited, he immersed himself in his academic career.

He began every semester with optimism and enthusiasm and scratched away his lonely evenings writing for prestigious journals, determined to ascend the University hierarchy. To date his greatest success had been "An Exploration of the Application of the Theory of Language Games to the Supreme Court Decision Making Process". When a couple of decades had dripped by like this and he had been polite to too many inferior colleagues who were awarded full professorships, he decided to distract himself by taking a summer European tour. It was an oversight that with his interests and opportunities, he had never been off the American continent. "It will do me good to hold my tongue and listen for a while, which is about all you can do when you don't know a language," he explained to sceptical friends.

Although it came at the tail end of a gruelling over-scheduled tour, he was so taken with Greece, that after a few visits he took a sabbatical from the University and moved to Athens to study and teach. He rented a tiny rooftop apartment that was more terrace than living space, that baked in the summer and froze in winter, but he was thrilled to have the opportunity to integrate his pet philosophies into the real world. For a few years his tiny flat was a pared down paradise at the centre of the philosophical universe until the noise and pollution drove him to look for a healthier option. This took the shape of his white box house at the top of a small village on a Greek island. He maintained his cheap Athens flat as a pied-a-terre. "I need to trade limited village life for an intellectual orgy once in a while," he'd say.

On one hot summer evening in the village, while sharing a large octopus he had caught with an American writer, he was introduced to a tall pale German woman in her mid thirties. She was a film producer who had been a sporadic visitor to the village for a few years. John knew her by name and reputation but was not prepared to meet someone that he couldn't keep his eyes off. Like she was one of his marine preys, he circled her for a while as she chatted and laughed with the other guests, and hoped she wouldn't notice him until his first few glasses of retsina had done their work.

"I hear you're a professor," she said when she caught him looking at her.

"Philosophy. Once upon a time," he said, "but let's not dwell on the barren heights of cleverness."

"In that case, come down to the green valleys of silliness," she answered. "Tell me something to make me laugh."

It had been a long time since John met anyone, especially a beautiful woman, who could quote

Wittgenstein. He was after all one of the pillars of modern philosophy.

"Sehr beeindruckend!" he said, and she did laugh, though he was not sure if she was surprised to hear him speak German, or if his pronunciation was very bad.

"I studied philosophy as well," she said, "but it wasn't for me. Movies were my first love. They were stronger than those dry intellectual gymnastics."

"Two things can connect," John suggested. "One can inform the other." To the exclusion of the other guests he dived into a discussion of how cinema could augment the principles of philosophy, and how his beloved Wittgenstein had loved movies, and even admitted that some of his ideas were suggested by things he had seen flickering across the black and white cinema screens of Vienna.

The dinner hostess, who had not played matchmaker intentionally, seated the new lovebirds beside each other. John mumbled and blushed his way through dinner, thrilled to find someone who was acquainted with his preferred subject.

"It's surprising we have never met," he said.

She stood up from the table and clanked a spoon against her glass. "A toast!" She waved her drinking arm in an arc to include everyone at dinner. "To old friends and to new ones." She directed her glass toward John. "To you."

"Prost!" he said.

"Come to see me in Munich," she said when she sat down. "I will find you something to do."

After she returned to Germany, they exchanged a few letters. Hers were short scrawled postcards from Rome, Madrid and London, and John's correspondence, because he saved his good paper for his essay submissions, were written in a tiny precise hand on butcher's paper that he had cut into envelope sized rectangles.

That winter, when the days were too cold to do much fishing, and John had been out the night before drinking more than was good for him, he would tell himself in the morning, "That's enough. No more booze." As the morning became midday and he felt worse, he would allow himself just one beer, some hair of the dog, but one always turned into more. If he didn't have more in the house, he would step out to buy a few more to get him through the evening. He tried to avoid the street with the taverna, but he wasn't always successful.

"Hey!" An English friend buying cigarettes at the kiosk in the square put his arm around John's shoulder. "Did you forget it's my birthday?" Of course, John couldn't refuse, everyone he knew would be there, a barbecue was laid on and so was the booze.

On the way home after another exaggerated night out, he fell down a set of steps he had barely managed to climb. In the morning he vaguely remembered falling. It might have been more than once, but it didn't matter because he had made it home. When he looked in the mirror to see why his face hurt, he was shocked to see it was scraped all down one side from the forehead to the chin. It stung when he cleaned it and as the day went on it settled into a stinging throbbing untouchable side of raw meat. He was tempted to have a beer to help with the pain but decided to go for painkillers instead. Not having a drink was a more difficult decision the next day, but he was too embarrassed to go out to buy anything. He'd wait until later in the week when he needed groceries, but then a friend stopped by and offered to shop for him. He didn't ask for alcohol. As his face healed, he thought or reasons to stay home and not be tempted by the taverna. "I have a paper to submit anyway and I need to be clear headed for that, so I'll wait," he'd say to himself. A week passed, his face was healed enough to venture out for shopping, and he was ready to talk about what he had done. There was sympathy but not too many questions. People knew he drank and fell down. That was John.

As the dry month went by his friends remarked how well he looked. They did what they could to protect him from himself and to shut down any well-meaning offers from strangers to have "just one." John realized he was not as strong as he wanted to be and appreciated the support from his friends. He was determined to make the abstinence permanent.

Late that winter Sabine returned to the village for a visit. "I have a proposal," she said. "In the spring I start a film in Munich and Switzerland. I'll find something for you. A small part if you want."

"For money or to be taken out in kind?" he joked. He wasn't desperate for the money because his father had recently died and left him a small inheritance. Anything he earned on top of that meant that he didn't have to dip into his principle. "As long as I don't play the fool," he said, but secretly he was overjoyed to be invited like it was his reward for good behaviour, his payoff for having pulled his life back together.

In March they started filming in Munich and as the cold weather retreated the production moved to an abandoned hotel outside of Davos. There wasn't time to play the tourist, so John spent his free moments getting to know the cast and crew. They were a mixed selection of educated, polite, intelligent, English speaking polymaths who could win at a scratch soccer game with the locals as well as create magic scenes with lighting techniques. Most had well informed opinions on all subjects, from art to politics, technology, engineering, history, language, and philosophy. They knew Wittgenstein and could recite passages from Hegel and Kant, rightfully proud of their important thinkers, familiar with this rarefied world in a way that opened John's eyes. His new acquaintances had incorporated the best elements of past philosophical systems into a coherent progression well enough to explain the highs and lows of the twentieth century. As well as intellectual talent, this gregarious group of working friends were full of creative energy, enthusiastic about putting in time day and night to capture magic on film. Not since he was a freshman at University had he experienced such a flush of being in a place he was born to inhabit. The possibility of a better world opened in front of him. He was a happy man. "My cup runneth over," he often said, half joking, stretching out his arms, palm upward like performing a Muslim prayer.

Although this new group of acquaintances understood most of his deeper philosophical tangents he sometimes felt set aside as an anachronism, though some of his apartness was related to language since he didn't speak fluent German. When he quoted Wittgenstein there was amusement and agreement if the epithet was timely, but their remarks implied that this particular branch of philosophy had done its time. "And so?" they would ask. "Where do we go from here?"

From the first night at Sabine's house in Munich, when they started the evening on the steel and leather sofa and ended up on the sheepskin rug with their hands and mouths all over each other, John and Sabine shared a bed.

"Why not?" She was as offhand as any young German about sexual relationships. "I am single, and you are the same, nobody gets hurt, it is just sex, we enjoy it, so let's do it!" She popped a dewy cherry into his mouth and held the stem as he plucked the fruit with his strong bright American teeth.

He was happy to fill his role as consort and for the opportunity to work with a talented group of people, a tight and mobile group of technicians whose work was to create art. "What have I been doing all my life?" he asked himself. He could have been a sound-man, a lighting designer, a cinematographer, an actor; it was all more exciting than academic life.

When filming was over it was an emotional send-off. Some of the group, including Sabine, were going on to other projects together, and others didn't know when they would see each other again. "I'm sorry." She held his hand across the breakfast table. "I'll only be in Japan for 6 months. We had a good time while it lasted, and we will see each other when I come back."

He returned to his small village, full of renewed energy and joyful to be home in his simpler world. He had no difficulty going down to pick up his post and drinking only a coffee at the taverna. He had no alcohol that entire winter and people stopped calling him Wheelbarrow John.

Early in spring he assembled his fishing gear on the beach at the start of the headland and noted with satisfaction that the sky had a high overcast, which was a good thing because fish saw shadows. The sea was very cold because it was still roughed up by late storms, but the wetsuit he had bought with some of his movie money would keep the chill away. Sabine was due to arrive for a few days at Easter and he planned to catch as many fish and octopus as possible to provide a bountiful feast. The film that John had worked on had been released and was getting a good amount of attention.

"I can't wait to spend Easter with you," he had written. "We can celebrate the rebirth of the neglected saviour. You know how much you excite me."

John waded backwards into the bay and was soon face down, snorkel up, kicking his way expertly around the base of the cliffs where the best fish hung out. He had only been out five minutes when he saw something move in an underwater crevice, so he dived down to investigate. As he peered into the gloom, a dog-faced animal shot out of the dark and collided with full force against his chest. It knocked his swim mask off and broke the strap on his spear gun sending it see-sawing down into the black depths. He kicked back to the surface and emerged with a gasp, controlling his breathing long enough to swim to the base of the cliff. After creeping with his hands along the jagged rocks for a few minutes he found a ledge large enough to pull himself out of the water. Once he caught his breath he began to cough and had trouble stopping each paroxysm. An unfamiliar taste crept onto the back of his tongue, and when he put his finger into his mouth, he saw that the spit had blood in it. He rinsed his hand in the cold turquoise water and touched his tongue again, but the blood was gone. He looked up and spotted a seal at a safe distance, treading water, looking back at him as if to say, "You're in my territory."

"Fuck you," John shouted which started him coughing again. The seal dived, leaving an empty sea, a calm expanse of steely water pressed against by a yellow-grey cloud that stretched all the way to the eastern horizon and the Holy Land.

It was a warm reunion with Sabine and her friends. There were hugs and kisses at the airport before they drove back to the village for a lamb dinner instead of the fish feast he had planned. Partway through the meal one of the guests, a French speaking journalist, got up to open another bottle of wine, and after she had poured Sabine's glass, she kissed her on the neck. Sabine turned and kissed the woman passionately on the mouth. John didn't stay long at dinner that night, but instead of going home his feet led him to the cafe and an ouzo. The drink tasted like gasoline but after the first sip he gulped it down and lurched out of the bar. He had almost made it home when he fell to his knees and started vomiting so strongly that it was like turning inside out. He sat slumped in a corner at the base of a long stone stairway, gagging and heaving until the tears and sobs took over. Home was so far away.

Sometime in midsummer the stomach pains started. At first, he thought they were from something he had eaten or came from drinking too much coffee, but after a particularly bad attack, clutching his hands to the side of his abdomen, he visited the local doctor. The doctor sent him to Athens for tests As instructed, he made the rounds of laboratories, but the attacks had stopped and he chastised himself for being a hypochondriac, so returned to his village to wait. One morning soon after, the telephone operator for the village came running to find him. "You have a call," he said. "From Athens."

"Cancer," the doctor said. "Lungs. You have maybe a year."

At first, he didn't tell anyone and carried on like nothing was wrong, but people began to comment that he was looking off colour and losing weight. "Lovesick," some said. "You need to get back with that German woman." He smiled at their concern and blamed his health on work and his meagre diet. He struggled to accept the idea that perhaps Sabine's company and that of her friends had been like a last ferry to the mainland and he had missed it. He had been presented with an opportunity to restart his life but had fallen back into his safe, solitary, regimented life so hadn't pursued it. Being nearly fifty was too old to start again. He would decide when he was better.

In the fall he moved to Athens, sceptical of the treatment the island doctor had prescribed. The days and nights of that winter were spent seeking warmth, shuffling from one cafe to another, reading, drinking metrio coffee, and stroking his long moustaches. The new treatment didn't work any better than the old one, and in February when the almonds were in bloom, he died in the multiple-bed oncological ward of a battered and understaffed Athens hospital.

The nurses didn't know what to do with the few things he left behind. He had been reading every day with his outsized tortoise glasses balanced on the end of his still elegant nose. Except for his misshapen glasses, the only personal items left behind were his well-thumbed Wittgenstein's TLP, and Hesiod's "Birth of the Gods", a classical Greek text with an embossed leather bookmark at the story of Pandora. A shaky hand had underlined a few lines of the text that suggested it was not the maligned Pandora, but her husband Epimetheus, the foolish brother of Prometheus, who had opened the forbidden jar. Epimetheus had since become known as the deity of people who realize things too late. None of the nurses could read the complicated English book or classical Greek so the indecipherable texts, not fit for the lending library, finished their well-thumbed lives in the hospital incinerator.

Tranquille

Mama did a lot of weeping and wailing when they took me away. She is normally a calm and collected person as you can tell by her sensible dresses, her sturdy shoes, and blunt-cut bobbed hair that turned white the year after she got married. My daddy more or less forced her to be the head of the household because he was a drinker. He worked at the lumber mill down by the river but sometimes he went missing for days when he was on a binge. Mama cried when the health department sent a car to take me to the sanatorium. The doctors told her that my condition was a risk to the public and that I would be lucky to come out alive.

I had apparently exhibited a classic symptom of my illness when I woke up one morning and saw my pyjama top covered in blood. I didn't feel sick at all, a little weak, but most mornings had been like that since the last time I had a cold. I had gone to my room early that night because I was tired and a bit sweaty, but I wasn't hurting at all. I must have coughed up the blood when I was asleep. I called mama and when she saw me lying in bed like that with my tongue out licking my bottom lip, she screamed. She must have thought I was dead, so I had to assure her that I wasn't.

The Tranquille Sanatorium is a quiet, friendly, medicinal smelling place, built for people like me. It opened twenty years ago as a two-storey, half-timbered main hall, with matching wings for the wards. There are as many south facing bay windows as the structure allows. The location had been chosen for its dry air and hours of sunshine because people like me don't do so well in the big cities down by the coast. We're better off in higher thinner air. The clay hills around us can only grow bunch grass, sagebrush, and a few gnarly pines so the whole area is classified as desert. Dry air is good for our condition.

People from the town nearby call the place The San. It sits on its own green delta that juts out into a long deep lake that generates offshore breezes to keep the hot summer air moving. In winter the shores of the lake freeze and local families come out in the crisp air to skate figures on the empty whiteness in front of the sanatorium. Even on the cold days the patients are wheeled out into the sun and covered in enough throws to keep them from getting chilled. They can see the skaters below, but no contact is allowed.

Just before I arrived, a new structure was added to the complex, so I was lucky enough to have a room in the tall cool San Diego style building with its red tile roof and blue striped awnings, more like a Florida resort than a sanatorium.

The treatment they gave me was the same they did for everyone. The doctors said that they caught things early, so my rehabilitation wouldn't take as long as it does for some. In the beginning while I was on strict bed rest, I heard the nurses and patients use shorthand terms for different stages of the cure. I was a Total, because I was on total bed rest. I wasn't tied down, but there was constant supervision to make sure that I didn't move. Getting up to go to the toilet wasn't allowed, there was a buzzer to push for help. I could only have bed baths to stay clean. If I was allowed to sit at all, they cranked up my bed and propped me at no more than forty-five degrees and lifted the side railings to make sure I didn't fall out. No deep breathing or excessive talking was allowed. The regime was a kind of torture but the promise of being allowed to get up and get out one day, left me no choice but to obey the rules.

Patients who were permitted to get out of bed to wash and use the toilet in their rooms were said to be on Washes, with the next step after that called S&B, for shower and bath. Being an S&B meant we could leave our rooms to use the public baths. This was a huge step because it meant that we could mix with the rest of the population, or at least those who were not in a contagious phase. Nobody knew each other; we were from all over. It was distant and superficial contact, but at least it was a taste of some kind of social life. We would joke that it was like being on a cruise except nobody was sure if, or when, they would get off the boat. We agreed that following the doctor's orders was the best policy if we didn't want to be wheeled out of our rooms in boxes.

I was still a long way from Washes and S&B and needed to learn some patience. Before I came here I would get angry if mama was late putting my dinner on the table, or my clothes weren't washed, but here I had no control over anything so I had to keep my temper down. The doctors said that if all went well, I would be able to get out of bed in a month, and that if my progress continued at the same rate I could be home in six months.

Hattie was the nurse who kept me on track. She was as upright as the starch in the collars of her tailored white uniform and as unapproachable as the bowed bib of the wrap-around apron that protected her from accidents. She was a tall strong woman who would probably come out on top if things got physical. I could imagine her having fights in bars except that nurses didn't do things like that. Her freshly polished white shoes and the two black bands on the wings of her nurse's cap signified that she was several steps above a regular nurse. She would fly in and out of my room like a levitating mother superior.

She is much bigger boned than my mother, who is even shorter than me, and she is certainly more commanding. When I'd ask if I could wear something else besides pyjamas, she'd answer the way my mother would, with a "We'll cross that bridge when we come to it." The commanding voice made her statements into orders, not at all like my mama's defeated vision of an obstacle-strewn future. Hattie was the only one who could have convinced me to stay in bed all day and night when I thought I would go crazy.

The doctors allowed me to keep my writing tools when I arrived, so I was able to maintain my correspondence. I had recently come to understand that there are many artistic souls like me out there with the same affliction. Some are famous and write back to me to tell me how they are getting along with their own illness and their latest works. Since face-to-face visits are forbidden, my literary friends are the only intellectual contact I have with the outside world. Dylan is the one I hear from most because he is a poet. I feel closest to him because he understands my ups and downs. George is the more prophetic and political of the two, so his words are much drier than Dylan's and mine. George helped me a lot by telling me that artistic souls like us need to stand up for each other because there are so many who want to tear us down. My literary friends live in Britain, so it takes a while for our letters to catch up with each other, but I don't mind waiting. What else am I doing? I do get a letter from mama once in a while, but she goes on and on about the garden, the weather, how many chickens she lost to wild dogs, and how much she misses daddy.

After a month I was officially allowed to sit up. Not exactly sitting but propped up like a pasha on an ottoman, waiting for the world to be served to him on a glittering plate. Hattie brought me my meals, washed me, dressed me and combed my hair because lifting my arms was still frowned on as an unnecessary strain on my chest. Rest and fresh air was the basis of my treatment. On sunny days, of which there were many, the nurses open the big windows in our rooms and wheel our beds near to them so we can get the maximum benefit of the champagne air.

When I finally graduated to Washes it was more difficult than I thought. I had been agitating to get out of bed for weeks, but it had been so long since I walked, that I had to spend half an hour with my legs hanging over the edge of the bed before I could put any weight on them. A physiotherapist showed up regularly to help start my muscles and walked with me for the first few steps to make sure I didn't fall over. It took almost a week, but with a couple of canes, I could put one foot in front of the other as many times as it took to get to the washroom and back. That short distance tired me out and Hattie scolded me for going too quickly but when they wheeled me out for my next set of tests they saw that I was still making progress, so they let me stay on Washes. Since I was no longer a Total, Hattie was assigned another couple of patients. She was probably overworked because she was not as helpful as she was when I was completely at her mercy.

Since I wasn't allowed out into the general population yet, Hattie brought me my meals, fixed my bed and made sure I managed my toilet safely. After a month of shuffling around my room with a cane, the doctor told me that I had graduated to Showers & Baths. I was thrilled to finally have a better look at the place they were keeping me. I remembered some of it from the day I arrived, but since then I hadn't seen anything except the pendant lamps hanging from the corniced hallway ceilings when they wheeled me out for tests.

There was no privacy in the public baths, but the attendants said it was for my own protection; that they didn't want me to drown with nobody there to rescue me. I was used to having my mama or Hattie outside the door if I needed to call for help, but here I had to take my bath in full view of the attendants. Although I wasn't happy with the idea, I had to accept that sometimes I needed people in exceptional circumstances.

The pleasure of fresh hot water rushing over me, making me clean everywhere, being dried off and wrapped in towels and housecoats and then instructed to spend the afternoon reclining in the solarium like royalty at a Czechoslovakian spa, was more refreshing than I could have ever imagined.

I was eager to have a look around the other wards, to see who else was in residence, but I could only manage it in brief increments. If I wanted to take a walk down the hallway, I had to choose my destination carefully because if I got too far away from my room to walk back, there would be a scolding from the nurse who had to rescue me with a wheelchair.

Once I was accustomed to being mobile, I spent more time out of my room, so I didn't see as much of Hattie. She sometimes poked her stern face around the door in the morning as if to say I've got my eye on you. And then she stopped visiting all together.

It was about that time that I had an unexpected relapse. One night I woke up feeling chilly and when I reached to pull up the covers, I noticed that my chest was wet. I called a nurse who turned on my night-light and saw that there was a huge wet stain of blood down the front of my pyjamas. That meant another stint of total bed rest for me, lying flat on my back again like a turtle who can't tip itself back the right way.

This time Hattie wasn't around to pamper me and I got instead a tiny little nurse called Betty. As much as Hattie was a battle-axe, Betty was like a ceramic doll equipped with batting eyelids and a mechanical giggle. Miraculously, in spite of her fragile appearance, she managed to get done what was needed. I was on my back for at least a week while they wheeled me back and forth for tests trying to figure out why I had a setback. While I waited for results, I was considered a Total again, confined to my bed. I would be monitored and probably graduate to Washes, and when I was strong enough, they would do a pneumothorax on me. It had been successful in cases like mine, but it meant collapsing one of my lungs to let it rest and then re-inflating it. "The disease needs oxygen to breathe," they said, "this will deprive it of sustenance."

When I finally had the operation, it wasn't as painful as I thought. They gave me a local anaesthetic so the doctor could put the needle into my lung and suck out the air. But during the night it hurt like hell and I had to call for Betty to give me something to relieve my pain. She did her best for me, but I was in a cranky mood most of the time and I probably ran her off her feet with my demands. I'm sure I made her cry, but I didn't care because I was not resigned to having to go through the whole round of treatment again. She wasn't like Hattie who would put me in my place and tell me to like it or lump it, but was full of apologies even though I asked her to do things that weren't on her list of duties. I told her she was too nice for her own good and made her cry again.

The lung collapse worked better than I thought because after a few more tests they let me go straight from Totals to S&B. Then, in a much faster time than anyone predicted I was on Walks. After that there was Work, which wasn't much more than helping in the dining room or attempting some light gardening, but most people had left the institution by the time they reached Work stage. They had homes, families and jobs that had been neglected for too long. The doctors said they weren't ready to let me go yet, and I was in no hurry to go back to mama's house.

Things were going well for me. I ate more than I had ever done, sat in the sun reading, writing, and being pampered like a millionaire. Soon I was allowed to dress in proper clothes and go to the patient's dining room to eat. This was too much for me at first with so many voices wanting attention. It upset my digestion. After trying it for a while, I asked to go back to eating my meals in my room, but this was against the institution rules. However, I threw enough food around that they relented and let me have my way.

My British friends were envious when they heard about me living the life of a lord while they scraped by as best they could without the appreciation they deserved. You wouldn't think that men so well known had to fret about the future, but it sounded like they had more worries than me.

Soon enough the bottom fell out of my world when nurse Betty went missing. The day she disappeared I had another relapse, just like my other episodes, waking up with my shirt covered in blood. They found Betty eventually in one of the tunnels that run between my building and the laundry. She was folded into a cupboard along with the body of a patient they thought had wandered off. For some reason, the police came to ask me questions, pressing for details about things I didn't remember. I don't know why they thought I had anything to do with her death because I was no different from any of the other patients, and here I was flat on my back and weak as a kitten. People said they had seen me with her, but stories get made up in a place like this where there is nothing better to do.

I heard talk of transferring me to another institution and I hoped it wasn't true because I had a demonstrated history of bouncing back to good health after some serious setbacks. A new nurse was assigned to me for my next term as a Total. Maybe they thought I had been too hard on Betty because this time the nurse was called Albert. In his white trousers and tight shirt, he looked like a muscle man who had been hired for his strength, not someone you talked back to without thinking. When he looked after me, there were a few things I went without because I didn't want to risk his disapproval or test the limits of his anger.

From what I heard, whiners got short shrift on his watch. You either needed something or you didn't; he was not prepared to run around after every whim.

I made it through Totals again and clocked up good progress on Washes because I wanted to work my way back to Walks that gave me the run of the place. As I progressed, I needed Albert less, though I know that he monitored every step of my recovery because he wrote it on the chart that was kept locked up at the main nurses station. Sometimes he had to come looking for me because I was not particularly bothered about dinner bells or curfews. I know this made him angry because he told me so. He had better behaved and more critical patients to think about.

There was something about Albert that I didn't trust, and I didn't think he trusted me. One day my instincts were proved correct when I came back from lunch and found him reading my correspondence. I had requested permission to have a locking briefcase for my writing so that nobody, not even Albert could look in. Some of the letters in there may have got me in trouble. Nothing I had written myself was in there as it had all been sent, but there were replies from my friends expressing their opinions about things that had happened here.

Dylan's last letter for instance contained a few lines about Betty. "It is difficult to be sure of the difference between illness and insanity," he wrote, "but considering the sins that have been committed, it is just as well that you are in a safe place, isolated from the rest of the world." I didn't need that kind of information getting out.

Albert would need to pay for his transgression. I had to find a way to get round his flank because he was too big and strong to be taken by surprise. I couldn't make him sick because he never ate or drank anything in my presence. I wrote to George for suggestions because he was the more practical of my correspondents, asking about how I might get this cumbersome white giant off my back. Albert was all over me like the plague, imagining that I had something to do with Betty's unfortunate disappearance.

When I returned to my room one afternoon and found him with my open locked briefcase bed in front of him, I rushed at him with what strength I had but of course he came out the better. I hadn't finished George's latest letter, so it hadn't been sent, and it was that very letter that Albert had in his hand. I thought he would strangle me then and there, but he relented when I started wheezing and coughing, something that people like me shouldn't do. He was angry that I was fighting him, so he strapped my hands and feet to my bed, threw my open briefcase on top of me, and wheeled me out the door across to the half-timbered main building, where he instructed the switchboard to call the supervisor.

I had to put up with the indignity of being gawked at by everyone, but that was forgotten when I saw the long-lost Hattie in all her white starchiness looming over me. She now had three black bands on her cap, which meant that she was the supervisor on duty for the entire institution.

"Well, well," she picked up some of the papers on my chest. "What has our naughty boy been up to?"

They left me lying there strapped to my bed on wheels and pushed into a corner, while they stepped away to exchange notes about me.

"I'll keep these letters," Hattie said when they returned. She was speaking to Albert, but she was looking at me.

"And it's back to the salt mines for you buster." She hit me on the shoulder with the sheaf of papers in her hand and lifted the briefcase of correspondence off my chest as Albert wheeled me away.

"Don't give him the benefit of the doubt!" she called as she strode straight-backed down the hallway to her desk. Once there, she slipped the incriminating letters into a file and locked them into a wall cabinet with the logo of the institution, THCI, Tranquille Hospital for the Criminally Insane.

Bedtime Stories

Isabel began parenthood determined to avoid using negative words with her children, but as they grew older it was more difficult to find creative ways to say no. Her friend Helen had no such scruples. On one occasion a few years earlier, Helen bit Isabel's son on the hand because he bit her first. Isabel was horrified but Helen insisted that he would never learn right from wrong if he didn't have firm guidelines. Still, Isabel did what she thought was right and shooed them out of the room if conversation took a turn towards sex or death. She was known to slap her hands over her children's ears if they walked into a room of adult talk, but the children had picked up more than she imagined and asked awkward questions, most of which she sidestepped, with a "Not now dear."

Helen had stopped by for a visit in mid afternoon and was still there at bedtime and when Isabel had tried sending the children off to bed with a quick hug and a kiss, but they hadn't settled down. "They're asking for you to tell them a bedtime story," she said, returning from her second trip to lay down the law.

"I'm not good at storytelling." Helen looked up from the diary that she had been updating while Isabel had been fussing with the kids. Helen was a precise woman, recording in detail every event and expense of the day.

"They said they will only go to sleep if you tell them a story." Isabel poured herself a cup of tea. Because she was English, tea was an all-day refreshment for her, though she could easily be talked into a glass of wine at any point from lunch onward. Helen hadn't done her the favour because she wasn't a wine drinker herself.

Isabel had come to Greece to visit a friend and stayed on to marry the village carpenter. In the early days of her marriage she spent most of her days at home with their two children, a girl and a boy who were now five and seven. Though her babies were now at school half the day she still had plenty to do, which apart from cooking and cleaning, laundry and shopping, meant looking after a menagerie of cats, chickens and the odd baby goat or lamb that her husband brought home. The old chapel and monastery where the family lived were at the head of a picturesque turquoise bay set against a dry landscape of orange and grey bedrock and prickly thorn bushes. It was a radical departure for an Ava Gardner look-alike from Islington who had been an art director at an advertising company in the city, but Isabel had been in love and had a stubborn streak beneath her sweet unfocused exterior. She hadn't counted on her husband being away from home so much. When he wasn't in his workshop crafting doors and windows, he was driving around in his pickup truck to check on the cattle that he kept as a sideline. Sustained by annual visits to London, Isabel was happy with her country life though she made rueful jokes about her husband's absences.

"I'd probably get more attention if I was a cow," she'd say. When grown-up company stopped by with news of the outside world, she was all ears, sad that she was missing out, but happy with her rustic life. Helen had taken up with her own Greek man at the same time as Isabel but it hadn't worked out so well for her. She closed her diary and stood up from the kitchen table. "I'll probably bore them to death but at least they'll go to sleep."

There were shouts of joy when Helen opened the bedroom door, so she started immediately into babysitter mode.

"Quiet!" she ordered. "Back into bed. Both of you."

"Please tell us a story," Anna looked up with her wide brown eyes. "Mummy said you would."

Helen sat down on the step of the wooden platform where the children slept on mattresses and leaned against one of the handrails that stopped them from rolling off the platform in the night. "I'm not good at fairy-tales," she said.

"Tell us something that has horses in it," Georgie sat forward and crawled to the end of his bed.

"Back under your covers," Helen pointed to his bed, "Or no stories."

"Tell us one about where you live!" Anna clapped.

"Let's see," Helen looked up at the hand-crafted coffered wood ceiling of the bedroom. "I can tell you about my Aunt Peggy, the one who loved horses. But the story probably won't put you to sleep, so when I'm finished you have to promise to go to sleep anyway." Both children clutched their winter duvets closer to their chests and nodded.

"A few years ago," Helen looked up at the wood squares on the ceiling, "my Uncle Bob had some heart trouble so had to stay in the hospital for a while. When he got sick, he and my Aunt were already separated, so my Aunt lived in their house in the country and my Uncle had an apartment in town."

"What do you mean separated?" Anna asked.

"Separated from each other silly," Georgie answered. He was two years older than his sister and proud of knowing more than her.

"They didn't get along, so they decided not to live together," Helen clarified.

"Can I get separated from Georgie?" Anna asked.

Georgie rolled his eyes.

"Did they have any children like us?" Anna asked to cover the retort she was about to receive from her brother for the first question.

"They had one", Helen said, "but by then he was grown up and lived with his girlfriend."

Anna nodded like it was something she already knew, but her big eyes showed that she didn't know such unusual living arrangements existed.

"After a couple of days of driving back and forth to the hospital, Aunt Peggy started to feel like she was coming down with a cold or the flu. Of course if she felt like that, she shouldn't have been going anywhere near a hospital should she, but she promised her ex that she would visit every day."

"What does X mean?" George piped up.

"X? Oh, ex. Ex-husband. Ex means something that used to be."

"Like the donkey we used to have?"

"Not exactly. The donkey died. Ex like this means he used to be her husband. So anyway, Aunt Peggy didn't stop to think that if her husband caught a cold when his heart was in such a delicate condition it could kill him. She told herself that she couldn't be sick, she didn't have time and she was just overtired from all of the driving to and from the hospital in the city. Her head was stuffed up and she was sleepy and sneezing but she needed to stay awake so she could get through the rest of the day. She dug through the bathroom medicine cabinet until she found some pills that her friend Emily had given her the last time she had a cold. After a few cups of coffee, she felt better, so decided that she didn't have anything wrong with her after all. Besides visiting Uncle Bob, she needed to go shopping because there wasn't any dog-food left in the house. For a few days she had been thawing out steaks from the freezer to feed her huskies who were happy to gobble down the meat, but the steaks were meant to be her own winter supply of protein

"When she got to the hospital, she realized that she'd mixed up her dates and this was the day her husband was supposed to have his heart surgery. There was barely time to give him a quick kiss before they wheeled him in. She had a lot to do, so as soon as the doors closed behind him, she took off to the mall to do her shopping. This took longer than she thought because she accidentally dropped her car keys into a bin of potatoes and the staff had to call out the produce manager to find them. Once she was done shopping she started to feel tired again, so took a few more of Emily's pills and went back to the hospital to wait for the results of her husband's operation and make sure that he was still alive."

"She stayed at the hospital that whole night in case he woke up and called out for her. He had been hurt in the war and sometimes he had nightmares, so she wanted to be there in case she needed to calm him down. In the morning he squeezed her hand and tried to say thanks, but his mouth was so dry he couldn't speak. She was sure she felt worse than he did because while he was snoring off the effects of the surgery, she had spent the night propped up in a chair in the waiting room more awake than asleep. Once she knew that he was all right and that the nurses would give him everything he needed, she took a couple of more pills for the way home. It had snowed during the night, so she bundled herself into a down jacket and went out in her tennis shoes to sweep the snow off her truck. She thought about staying in town with her sister, my mother, but after her long night in the uncomfortable chair she could only think about her bed at home. She had to get home in any case because the animals needed feeding. They count on us, don't they?"

The children nodded.

"And she had a few animals to take care of," Helen said. "Three Yorkshire terriers, two husky dogs, two cats, a budgie and three horses that all needed feeding every day. She couldn't leave the house empty for too long in winter because the pipes might freeze. The heating was already on its lowest setting to save on having to refill the big propane tank in the yard. It had to last until spring because she didn't have the money for more propane when it ran out. When she was at home, she lit the wood fireplace for heat and if it was really cold she turned on the gas oven and opened the door. People told her using the gas oven was the same as turning up the furnace, but she didn't believe them."

"Aunt Peggy had always been crazy about animals, so when she split up from Uncle Bob, she wanted to keep the house in the country because that's where the animals lived. When they were still married they had two cars, but when he moved out he kept the Cadillac and she got the old truck because she needed a truck to bring home hay for the horses.

"So, there she was in the hospital parking lot the morning after Uncle Bob's operation, sweeping the snow off her car with a broom she borrowed from a janitor. When she was done and got the truck started she was so steamy and sweaty from the snow clearing that the windows fogged up immediately. She put the heater and defroster on high and drove away as slow as the car would go. Other drivers honked at her if she steered onto their side of the road, but she didn't care because she was concentrated on not sliding on the ice. It wasn't an easy drive because the front window was still mostly frozen except for a small space above the steering wheel, and because it was morning, she was driving into the sunrise and the bright light made her eyes want to close. She had made the hospital trip so many times that the truck practically knew the way home by itself. When she got off the main highway, she relaxed a bit because there was less traffic; the truck was finally warm, and the windows were clear.

"When she was almost home, she noticed that there were horses running beside her truck and she was surprised when one of them ran out in front of her. A couple of the ones beside her peeled off down side roads, but this one horse galloped in front of the car all the way home. She imagined the horses were feeling frisky because it was such a beautiful crisp winter morning.

"When she went up her driveway her own horses started to act the same, running up and down the pasture and kicking out if the other horses came too close. Maybe they were hungrier than she thought but they didn't usually behave like this when she came home. She parked by the front porch and lugged the shopping into the house, desperate to go to bed, but she couldn't sleep yet because the horses needed feeding."

"We have to do that too, don't we?" Anna said.

"That's right, Helen answered, "only you have cats and dogs, and goats and chickens instead of dogs and horses."

Helen went on with her story. "Aunt Peggy changed out of her good clothes into her country clothes which were usually a pink fluffy housecoat, one of Uncle Bob's down jackets and a pair of gumboots. When she shuffled across the top of the driveway on the way to get hay for the horses, she noticed a tangled mess of something halfway down the driveway but didn't look too hard at it because she had more important things to do than cleaning up the yard. The horses were back to their calm selves when she threw hay over the fence for them. The dogs got some real tinned dog-food for breakfast but the cats had to share a couple of chunks of frozen liver. When all the animals were fed, she stacked some logs onto the fire, kicked off her boots and pulled a blanket over herself on the couch and fell into a deep sleep.

"Around noon a loud crash from the kitchen woke her up. When she stepped off the sofa, one of her Yorkshire terriers was under her foot so instead of standing up and crushing it, she fell face down on the rug. After she made sure she hadn't broken any of the dog's tiny bones, she went round to the kitchen and saw that the cats had ripped a hole in one of the shopping bags she left on the table. They had pulled a bag of shrimp out and were chomping on them with the shrimp tails sticking out of their mouths. Most of the shopping was on the kitchen floor, including a jar of pickles that broke and soaked everything with brine and glass. That's probably what woke her up. She was standing there swearing at the cats and wondering where to start to clean up the mess, when there was a banging on the door beside her that made her jump a mile. She looked out the peephole and saw that it was Emily's husband. He shouted to ask if she was all right. "Why?" she shouted back, but then thought that was rude so she opened the door and asked him again to his face. He told her that somebody had a bad wipeout down the road that morning. A car had gone off into the ditch and ripped out half of his front fence. His horses got out and he was still looking for one of them. He pointed to her truck and said that he noticed a bunch of wire in her driveway, and when he got closer, he saw that there was a lot of wire wound around her axle. The posts strewn down the driveway looked to him like they came from his fence. Peggy stepped out onto the porch and had to squint to make out a trail of debris on the driveway. She swore she didn't know how they got there because she had been at the hospital all night.

"Luckily Emily was a good friend of Aunt Peggy's and knew what she was going through, so convinced her husband to come back later to cut the wire off Peggy's axle so she could drive to the hospital again if she needed to. Aunt Peggy was too embarrassed to watch him work in the cold and snow so she went back to sleep on the sofa and didn't wake up until it was cold and dark and too late to visit her ex husband.

"People told her later that they had seen the wheel tracks of the vehicle that had ripped out Emily's fence. And there was the tangled heap of wood and barbed wire that had been left in her yard because it couldn't be re-used. Although she couldn't remember it, she must have fallen asleep and the truck drifted off into the ditch and carried on for a while before it started knocking down the fence posts. They said it was lucky that where she left the road was in a field because further on she would have hit a tree for sure. It had been Emily's horses who were terrified of the clattering string of posts whipping around behind Aunt Peggy's truck like a tail of tin cans on a newlywed's car. They found the missing horse the next day making itself at home at somebody else's haystack. Aunt Peggy threw out the rest of Emily's pills and blamed them for the accident."

"What were they?" Georgie asked.

"The pills? Probably just Contac C."

"Is that like LSD?" Georgie asked. "Mummy doesn't let us take pills."

"I should hope not."

"What did Uncle Bob say?" Georgie asked, guessing that there would be some kind of father figure punishment.

"Oh," Helen said. "He died a couple of weeks after. Of an infection."

Both the children were silent.

"Was he old?" Georgie asked.

"Not really," Helen said. "Too young to die."

There was more silence from the children. Matter of fact death was something they had seen in the animal world but hadn't made the connection with anyone they knew. Uncle Bob was a stranger to them, but he was a person, not a chicken who had wandered onto the road and been hit by a car.

"Tell us another story." Anna scrunched down in her bed with the covers pulled up to her chin. "A funny one."

"A quick one," Helen said. "It's getting late and you need to go to sleep. Let me see," she said and looked up at the ceiling. "How about the switch in the apple tree?"

"What's a switch?" Georgie asked.

"Wait and see," Helen said. "This one is about Aunt Peggy too, when she was still married. Uncle Bob was a real estate agent and she thought she could be one too. Everyone was surprised when she passed all the tests; she wasn't the smartest in her family. One of the most important things Aunt Peggy learned in her new job was how important it was to make a good impression on her clients. Luckily, she loved clothes and was always dressed elegantly, but her professional career gave her a reason to make her everyday wear special. She had also discovered that she was more likely to make a sale if her clients were unaccompanied men because she could put her beauty and charm to work on them.

"One Saturday she had an appointment with an especially handsome man, so she did herself up in seamed stockings, high heels, a form fitting dress, dangling earrings, full makeup and a hairpiece pinned to the crown and back of her head to make a French roll. A fake ponytail of hair like that is what we call a switch.

"She was proud of herself that she could answer the man's questions about the heating and cooling, property taxes and mortgage rates. When the handsome man suggested they go out to the back garden to look at the roof of the house, she followed him to answer more questions. When he stepped onto the back lawn she walked after him, but her high heels sunk into the soft grass. She couldn't follow him all the way because her shoes were stuck but she tried not to let on that anything was wrong. She batted her eyelids and looked over at him as he mentioned the peeling paint on the back of the house and the missing bricks from the chimney, and hoped that he would walk away so she could pull her heels out of the wet grass. She answered as best she could that the defects were nothing serious and as she did so, the man approached her and reached his hand toward her shoulder. She thought he was about to touch her so jerked her head away and tried to step sideways but forgot that her shoes were stuck. To avoid falling over she stepped out of one of her shoes and the soggy wetness immediately soaked through her best stockings. The man briefly looked down but didn't say anything and reached toward her again, so she stepped out of the other shoe and smiling slightly like nothing was wrong, she moved a few feet away. She was sorry her stockings were wet, but it was probably better than letting a man she didn't know put his hands on her. She was unsure whether to grab her shoes and run or to make a joke about what was happening.

"The man reached out again but not toward her this time, because he poked at something hanging on the branch of an apple tree. At first she thought it was a cat, but it was too small, maybe a kitten, maybe a rat. While she tugged her high heels out of the wet ground, the man grabbed for the thing in the tree, twisted it and turned it and eventually got it off the branch. Back on the brick patio behind the house, she wiggled her feet into her dirty shoes, and the man walked toward her with his hand over whatever he had plucked from the tree. She had no intention of even looking at it, but when he held it out to her she backed away, laughing a bit because she was embarrassed, but frightened of whatever he was trying to give her. He tried to tell her that it belonged to her, but she shook her head to say no and hardly glanced at the brown lump he held in his open hand. Something about it looked familiar, a few single strands of auburn sunrise, and when her hand went to the back of her head to check, all she could feel where her hairpiece had been were bobby pins and empty space.

"She didn't admit it was hers and told the man to throw the nasty thing into a garbage by the back shed. She finished up with him faster than she intended because she didn't want to turn her back to him so he could see the place where the switch had been attached. After he left, she went out to the garbage at the back to see if her switch was worth rescuing, and there it was looking like a dead hedgehog at the bottom of the empty bin. When she gingerly reached down for it, she thought she heard her mother's voice tell her something she had heard many times as a child. 'You brought this on yourself, young lady,' the voice said. "

"Mummy says that too," Anna said quietly.

"And she's right, "Helen answered. "When first we practice to deceive."

"What does deceive mean?" Anna asked.

"It means to tell a lie," Helen explained. "To fool people into thinking something is real when it's not."

Little Anna stroked her lips with a finger as she tried to think the concept through. "Are braids a lie?" she asked hesitantly as if she had already committed the sin.

"No," Helen said. "Because they're part of you. But that's enough for tonight kids. Sweet dreams."

She tucked the two wide-eyed children in and turned out the bedside light. When she stepped out into the glare of the gas light in the kitchen, Isabel was still cradling a mug of tea at the table.

"Thanks," she said. "Sounds like they've gone off to sleep."

"Maybe not," Helen said, "but I think they'll be quiet." She accepted a cup of tea from Isabel to refresh her throat that was parched from so much talking. She smiled to herself, pleased to have been a secret agent of subversion. Her tea was bitter so she added a spoonful of honey and stirred it idly, remembering the church bells she had heard earlier in the village that were the reason for her escape to Isabel's place in the country.

Helen had flown across the world to see her boyfriend for ten years running, but he had never told her he would marry her. It was just as well they didn't have children considering how things had gone. She thought Isabel had been precipitous and foolish when she first got pregnant. And now, staying in the village was impossible on his wedding day, being looked on with pity while her boyfriend married the daughter of a shop owner. Isabel was on her side and didn't think much of the chosen wife either. Helen had a quick flash of remorse, wondering if Isabel's children would have sweet dreams or wake up screaming about wild horses and car accidents, or rats on their heads. It would serve their mother right for keeping them so isolated from the dark realities of life. Helen was of the firm opinion that fairy tales accustom children to the idea that bad things happen, and the sooner they learn it the better.

Canadian Thanksgiving

In spite of centuries of bickering about the right or wrong of Thanksgiving, it was Bill's favourite holiday. Canadian Thanksgiving was a month earlier than the American one, so the weather was often better. He had been on a hike that morning with a friend, and had sunk into the sofa to watch a football game, or what was left of it by the time his household chores were out of the way.

Nancy appeared from the kitchen. "Get your feet off the coffee table." She pointed with the wooden spoon in her hand.

Bill thumped his crossed feet down onto the rug.

"I forgot to buy Coke," she said. "Patric only drinks rum these days and I told him we had the mix."

"Do you need it now?" he asked without taking his eyes off the television. He knew that his wife was nervous about dinner even though the guests were her own children. Their son Patric was away at University in

Montreal. "He's not even here yet," Bill said, knowing he was being difficult but also that peace at home superseded football. He had been married to Nancy long enough to know that her agitation was concealed excitement. She was cooking the big meal so it was fair he should do his duty as a last-minute delivery service.

"What time will he be here?" He punched his arms into the sleeves of an inside out jacket.

"Becca should be here first. Roy's picking her up from the airport."

Their daughter Rebecca was a nurse a Vancouver General.

"Who's Roy?" Bill asked

"Her new boyfriend. The one who was in Peru?"

"Remind me again why Peru?"

"He's a dentist honey," she said. "He gives up his vacation to help out down there."

"Oh, Jeez," Bill rolled his eyes. "A do-gooder. A tree hugger." He had already decided not to warm to this boyfriend. His daughter was an adult, but he didn't think she understood men well enough yet to settle down with one. Being a grandfather was on his wish list, but he was not in a hurry for his baby to start having babies. It would be easier to accept if his son was a father.

When he returned from the corner store, a car he didn't recognize was parked in front of the house, and a taxi that had probably dropped off his son was pulling away. The arrivals were shedding coats and giving hugs when Bill walked in and through the flurry of upraised sleeves, shoulders, and waving arms he picked out his daughter. With her straight blonde hair, strong brows and wide intelligent eyes, she was the same princess who had always rushed into his arms and she didn't disappoint him this time as she jumped off her feet to give him a hug. He hoped he hadn't made her into too much of a tomboy. He was never big on girlish pursuits so had taken both of his children to football games, on fishing trips, horseback riding in summer, and skiing in winter. His daughter had even taken up wrestling in her teens just because he had taken an interest in Olympic wrestling for a while himself.

When the hugs were over, Becca introduced him to Roy, who stood aside with a slight smile and observed the family greetings. He was taller, thinner, and older than Bill expected, in his early thirties with short dark curly hair and oblong-framed glasses. He wore a crisp white shirt, a black waistcoat and dark blue jeans. He reminded Bill of his father when he was young. When they shook hands, the young man held his hand with a strong grip and didn't let go. Bill looked up into the other man's eyes, which studied him as if trying to read something about his daughter, but their eyes stayed locked for a few seconds too long. The blood rushed to Bill's face and he pulled his hand away as if it had been burned. The spark that had flashed between them wasn't curiosity but recognition.

Grasping for something to say to cover his rudeness, Bill backed toward the kitchen. "How about a beer?" he ventured, looking only obliquely at the other man. His mind shifted into overdrive trying to remember where he knew this supposed stranger from, but the only picture that jumped into his head was of the two of them kissing. "No, no, no," he muttered.

"Pardon me?" Roy looked inquisitive, like nothing had happened.

"What?" Bill had forgotten what he was doing.

"What've you got?" Roy asked.

Bill looked up blankly at the bright smile.

"Beer," Roy reminded him.

"Oh. Right. Beer." Once he could focus on his mission, he adjourned to the bustle of the kitchen to catch his breath and he called from there, "Becks or some local brew?"

"How local?" Roy was at the kitchen door.

To avoid any more searching looks, Bill frowned into the fridge. "The beer up here isn't my own if that's what you're asking." The other man's presence made him uncomfortable, so he fell back on nervous chat. "I like craft brew but that's all downstairs" he said. "I'll show you later."

What the hell was he doing? He had just invited this man who had turned him into a stuttering fool to go downstairs with him. He hoped the offer would be forgotten in the course of the evening. The visitor had risk written all over him and one mistake would be very bad for his secret life of half-truths.

"I'll take the Becks," Roy said. "Maybe I'll try one of your special ones later." Bill suspected the young man was onto him.

As they were about to sit down for dinner, he disrupted his wife's seating arrangements by insisting that his son take the chair on his left. Bill's wife was at his right hand as usual. His son however, didn't want to sit beside his father, which led to one of their inevitable raised-voice fencing matches. Bill didn't particularly want to sit beside his son either but wanted to be as far away as possible from the new boyfriend. Perhaps his show of being the gruff father would make the visitor think twice before he took any liberties. His wife smoothed things over as she always did, while his daughter gave him a pleading look from the end of the table that told him not to make a scene.

When everyone was seated, Bill silenced them for a toast to give thanks for family, home, health, good fortune, and good company. As the family sipped from their glasses and began to fill their plates with squash and potatoes, Bill deftly manipulated the point of the outsized carving knife between the drumsticks and thighs to separate them. He silently gave his own thanks for mornings like the one he had just spent with his friend Mal.

He and Mal had set off early that morning, taking a trail up Mount Work that snaked through fissures in the bedrock, and over tussocks of moss that were pearled with dew in places where the sun hadn't shone. Further on they picked their way over barriers of windfalls on a densely timbered trail, across bands of gravel scree, until they scrambled on all fours up the steepest part of an outcrop of crumbling rock to an alpine meadow, where the sun bathed the grassy knoll of the summit. As they scanned the dense forest of Douglas Fir below and looked out across the Salish Sea to the Olympic Range where a skiff of fresh snow had added a frosted topping to the distant mountains, Mal put his arm over Bill's shoulders. "We should do this every day, buddy," he said.

The friends had met at a gym a few years earlier, where a few chats in passing had turned into visits to a coffee shop after every workout. Mal was a mature fitness enthusiast. He never missed an occasion to run up and down stairs instead of using the elevator, entered races appropriate for his age group, and in winter played with an old timers hockey league. At the gym he was a rib puncher, a butt grabber, and a wet towel snapper. Bill had grown up in a family of brothers and had played football in high school, so he understood Mal's type of uncomplicated camaraderie. Mal was someone who pushed Bill to get what little exercise he did.

Both men were approaching fifty and had adult children who no longer lived at home. Locker room banter sometimes turned to the subject of sex, and they both joked about going without sex for too long. Each had started his married life having sex at least once a day, but things had changed over the years so now they were down to once a week if their wives would allow it. They had joked about masturbation, both admitted to doing it and had some good laughs swapping stories about what they had done out of boredom. Between family and work schedules they managed a hike once a month and had been lucky today because the weather was superb, though weather was rarely a factor since they didn't go on their outings just for the exercise.

Once they had caught their breath from the climb and taken a few photos for proof of their accomplishment they sat down to eat a snack.

"Anything interesting?" Bill asked. He had brought a cheese sandwich he had thrown together early that morning and was hoping that Mal had brought something sweet. Bill was on strict instructions from his wife not to eat anything with sugar because it was like poison to him, but his sweet tooth hadn't gone away, and he figured that a cheat here and there wouldn't hurt anyone.

"I have a truckload of these cookies," Mal pulled a zip-lock bag out of his knapsack. "Homemade. Hard as a rock."

When they had finished their snack and were on their feet again, Mal asked, "Where should we go?"

"It's quiet up here right now," Bill turned around full circle. "I'd like to be in the sun, so I was thinking down that direction." They had climbed up the main trail on the west side of the mountain and he pointed south. Halfway down to the arbutus edge of the tree line and out of sight of the summit, they found a warm place at the foot of a small bluff.

"I've been waiting for this all week," Mal stripped off his shorts over his hiking boots. His windbreaker and t-shirt came off over his head and he held his arms outstretched toward the view in front of him.

"You'd better be careful a Sasquatch doesn't come out of the woods down there and grab your goodies," Bill laughed. Now naked himself, he came up behind Mal, hugged him and ran his hands down the front of his friend's body. Mal turned to face him they pressed their naked torsos together, breathing in the scent of each other at close range. They didn't kiss; Mal didn't like that.

"Who's up first?" Bill said.

"I'm still hungry", Mal smiled and knelt down in front of his friend.

Because they had been hiking together for a few years they knew how to push and tease each other to satisfaction. Afterwards they lay face down, side by side on the moss in the sun.

Years earlier when Bill first began making contact with men for sex, he asked himself if he was bisexual or even gay, but he decided that the question didn't need a definitive conclusion. He was not attracted to boyish or feminine men. If he wanted the attention of a woman, he had a perfectly feminine wife at home, so his taste ran to masculine men who didn't want commitments, dramas, or complications. He stopped looking for labels and accepted his desire to meet up with men as part of his nature, even if it didn't jibe with his matrimonial situation.

Bill had almost fallen asleep when he was startled awake by a slap on one of his bare butt cheeks. "Time to go buddy." Mal had already pulled on his shorts. They took a roundabout trail back down the mountain so they could have more time to talk about the things they didn't bring up at home, like other married men who chased women on the side and about European men who had mistresses and that their society didn't fall apart because of it. Bill had discovered early in his marriage that playing with women could be disruptive to his home life. In exchange for sex, other women wanted things he wasn't prepared to give. Men were satisfied with anonymous contacts, chasing pleasure for its own sake, pleasure that didn't require money, emotional commitment or fidelity. His secret life kept him happy at home because it satisfied his need for male company. Other men had sports, he had sex. If his hobbies were contrary to the prevailing moral weather, that was not his problem.

"How was your hike today?" his wife asked when they were halfway through their Thanksgiving dinner.

"Good. Great." Bill swallowed a big mouthful. "We took the long way back down through the bog. I think I still have a few Devil's Club spines in my shorts."

"How is...what's your friend's name.... Mel?"

"Mal. Malcolm. He's fine. His kids are coming down from up-island tonight."

She didn't usually ask about his friends because if she interrogated him it usually ended in an argument. He told her what she needed to know, told her when and where he was going, whether for a beer, to a hockey game, or on a hike. Nancy rarely remembered his friends' names but Mal had been on the scene for a few years.

"We should all go on a hike together one day," she looked around the table.

Bill stopped eating. "Mal's a fast walker," he said. "You'd be running to keep up. Besides, it's our decompression time."

"Decompression from what?" she asked.

"Work," he said and with his teeth pulled the meat off a drumstick he held in one hand. She blinked and paused as if she was about to take up the thread, but instead looked down at a piece of skinless turkey breast on her plate, continued to saw through it with a blunt knife and was silent.

In the beginning Bill and Nancy had sworn a pact of honesty, but after he confessed to a few calls with infidelity, he discovered that the naked truth wasn't always appreciated. They had also talked about having an open marriage, but it was always Nancy, sometimes at the last minute, who backed away from these arrangements. After a few years of marriage and a few children, Bill realized that the difference in their sexual energies had grown from an inconsequential wrinkle to an empty ocean. While the children were growing up he kept to his wife's schedule and denied himself, but underneath there was a hunger that existed and wanted to be satisfied. Once he decided to follow that old instinct, he was astonished to discover that in his city there was a vast underground of men like him, middle aged men in relationships with lives they didn't want to abandon, but who needed more than they were getting at home. Always worried about bringing some disease home, Bill reduced his risk by only meeting up with married men like himself. Of course, things had happened. One day he discovered there were crab lice crawling around his private parts, so he immediately hit the drug store, the shower, the washing machine and a fine comb to take care of any lingering traces. There were a few scares with urinary infections, but he had feigned being under the weather as a way to work around his wife's weekly sexual schedule. It was a risky game, but he reasoned that life was dangerous, so he would deal with the consequences if and when they arrived.

White lies were the lubricant of social intercourse, but they also greased the cogs of compromise that were necessary for long term cohabitation. The benefit he gained from his secret life was worth the invisible stain on his perceived reputation as a good husband, father, and provider. He had been present and loving with his children and seen them through childhood illnesses, broken bones, and the dramas of adolescence, patient with the them and the duties of hearth and home because they brought him things he also wanted. He had willingly done all in his power for his family because he loved them as much as his own life. He still loved his wife and wanted to live with her to the end, but after so many years of dealing with daily necessities, their connection had lost some of its spark. On occasion they could find it again, but it wasn't as overwhelming and all consuming as it had been at the start. They were friends; they were accustomed to each other and didn't want to contemplate a future of living apart. Up to now they had lived a happy, fulfilled, though routine life. It would be a tragedy to throw it up in the air.

"Dad. Dad!" It was his daughter's voice.

He looked up, surprised to find himself still at the dinner table pushing a last half of a Brussels sprout round his plate.

"Are you going deaf in your old age?" she asked. "Roy asked you a question."

"Oh. Sorry," Bill muttered. "I had my mind on something else."

"You work too much dear," his wife said.

"What was it he asked?" Bill squinted and tipped his head so he couldn't see the new boyfriend too clearly.

"Beer," Roy said. "I wouldn't mind one of those special beers of yours."

Damn! The pit opened in front of Bill and he knew if he were alone in the cellar with this man, who radiated sparks of testosterone and wry good humour, he would be tempted to give himself away. As he led the way downstairs, he reminded himself to keep his eyes, thoughts, and hands to himself.

"My workshop." He indicated the double-sided workbench that filled the extra parking space in a two-car garage. The wall along that side of the workshop was floor to ceiling cupboards, and when Bill opened one of the lower sets a refrigerator with a glass door revealed itself. "Any preference?" he asked.

"You choose," Roy said. "Something you think I'd like."

Bill stooped to pick out a green bottle. "Steam Whistle," he read from the label. "A pilsner, lots of head."

"Do you think I'll like it?" Roy asked.

"Here." Bill held out the bottle to the other man who grasped both the bottle and the hand that was holding it. "You need to drink it in a glass," Bill tried to pull his hand away. "We'll take them upstairs," he tried again, but the man's hand still held him. He looked up into the other man's smiling eyes and didn't move when Roy leaned in to kiss him on the lips. It wasn't a friendly peck but the start of a passionate kiss. Bill pulled himself away and wiped the back of his hand across his lips. "No," he said. "No." Going further would be dangerous for both of them, though he realized immediately that Roy wasn't likely to tell anyone since he had made the first move. "Not here," he said, aware he had admitted to himself and the other man that he was willing to give in to temptation. The danger of the game sent a rush of adrenaline deep into his bones.

He was long past believing that a thunderbolt from God would strike him down for his sins. It was like he had a passion for a particular food that common knowledge indicates is poisonous, but he had discovered that it wasn't poisonous for him. During his adult life he had learned to blend disparate elements of his character into a whole, and integrate his sexual schizophrenia into a way of life that worked for him. It was a delicate balance that was based on secrecy. For his sin of omission, he didn't believe he was going to hell. He was a good man and a good husband and if God existed, he would know that no man was perfect.

But Bill knew that God was dead, and he was not controlled by a canon of perverse and supernatural prophets and saints. Life was all in the joy of the moment, not about dragging a moral ball and chain through paradise. Patriarchal laws were in decline thanks to medicine and birth control. If women decided to have sex outside of matrimony there were no longer life changing consequences for them, and by default men were also freed.

Bill had no intention of arriving at the end of his life reciting a rosary of missed opportunities. Though his chosen road was contrary to popular morals, he took the obstacles as challenges rather than impediments. If Nancy ever found out and confronted him with proof of his underground life, he would deny it. The other man had instigated it, he was curious, it was a one-time thing, he didn't know what had come over him; a plausible story was required because he had no intention of stopping. Discovery would only mean that he needed to be more careful.

As they climbed the stairs back to the dining room, each carrying his unopened bottle of beer, Roy led the way. From behind Bill gave him a hard smack on the butt, something his gym buddy Mal would have done. When they returned to the dining room with their foaming beer freshly decanted into glasses, they were flushed and laughing like the best of friends. The family looked up from the dinner table with puzzled relief, happy to see there had been an unexpected change in the weather.

"There you are!" Nancy said. "We thought we'd lost you."

Hotel Chronicles

Monday

Gabi the head housekeeper reports that the parents of a boy's lacrosse team who stayed in the hotel on the weekend put their kids to bed in the evening then pulled room chairs out into the hallway and had a party. They spilled beer on the carpet and sprayed it up the walls.

"Those parents are more badly educated than the children," she says in Italian accented English. "Maleducati! Totally without manners."

Nora, the front desk manager, comes to the office to report that other guests had problems with the group. At checkout, Nora had brought up the issue of a noise complaint with one of the mothers of the team and was told, "Wait until you have your own kids. That'll wipe that stupid smile off your face." Nora straightens the company blazer that she is required to wear as a uniform. It's tailored fit gives her power. The way she buttons it up and undoes it gives the manager some access to her state of mind, and this time her nervous fingers twist the buttons like she wants to pull them off.

Fred the night clerk has written a lengthy message to say he offered the unruly parents an empty banquet room, but they insisted that they couldn't move away from their sleeping children. "I have rarely encountered," he wrote, "such boorish behaviour on the part of supposedly decent people. They were drunk and rude. One of them called me a pimple-headed pussy. I should not be subject to such insults."

Megan in Sales is requested to dig through her contracts to find the team organizer's credit card number and call them to inform them of the cost of cleaning up the mess, but she can't put her finger on a copy of the contract. Her desk is a snow-capped mountain of unfiled documents that she has not taken the time to organize.

Klaus the maintenance man stops by to report that he has recovered twenty empty beer cans from the roof of the restaurant. "Jeez," his big voice booms out. The manager puts up his hands and points to the open door, but Klaus doesn't understand the signal to close it. "Those fuckers went through a shitload of beer," he says with a note of admiration in his voice.

Before Klaus leaves the manager's office he overhears a call from the front desk reporting that there is an unknown person in the banquet room helping herself to the buffet lunch that has been laid out for a conference of indigenous women. The organizer says that she is not part of their group, for starters she is not native, and nobody knows her. Klaus, in his airforce-blue boiler suit, catapults himself up from his chair and in a few strides is halfway down the hall shouting, "I'll show that freeloading bitch the door."

"Gently!" the manager calls after him.

Looking over the weekend statistics, the manager notices there are a few room accounts seriously in arrears. Nora the front office manager with her breezy pageboy haircut is summoned to explain why.

"Don't tell me that scruffy guy down the hall is still here?" the manager asks.

"The last manager did all that Sir. The welfare department promised us rent, but now they're giving us the run-around."

"When was the last time he paid?" The manager flipped through a few pages on his desk.

"He gave us some a while back Sir. Every week he says the money will be here any day, but we haven't seen much. He's two months behind. I think he's spending his rent money on booze, "

"Kick him out." The manager turns to the next account. "We'll fight with the government later."

Growing up in a Newfoundland fishing village, Nora has a distaste for dishonesty. She is polite and agreeable with all of the guests and gives them the benefit of the doubt but in a case like this where she thinks she is being taken for a fool, she is happy to carry out the manager's orders.

The manager flips over more pages on his desk. "Sylvia's late again." He holds out a room folio at arms length as if it smells bad. "You need to do something." He rattles the paper in Nora's direction so she will take it away. Sylvia Phillips checked in two months earlier with stated intentions of staying a week, but she is still in residence.

"We know she's got money Sir. She has her own house in the swanky part of town." Nora has done her homework. "When we ask her for rent, off she goes to see her lawyer, dressed like she's going to have breakfast with Audrey Hepburn. The girls tell me them pearls she wears are real. She never comes back with much 'cept the rent cheque and a little string bag of biscuits."

"Why the hell doesn't she stay at home?" The manager frowns, although he is long past trying to understand people's motives.

"Her own mum and dad were here a few times. They drive this big old English car. A Benson?"

"Bentley," the manager corrects. "I don't care if they drive a Ferrari or a kiddie car. She owes us money." He raises an eyebrow at Nora. "And don't forget young woman, that a night's sleep is not returnable merchandise. Stay without pay is a crime."

"Yes Sir," she bows her head and scribbles a note. "I'll send her a letter."

"Make it an ultimatum," the manager says.

Klaus returns to the manager's office to report that he has evicted the freeloader from the banquet room. "She was a mouthy fucker," he says. "Told me that the lobby was a public place, and she could stay there as long as she liked."

Klaus, all two meters of him, had frog marched the offender out of the front door but she hung around at the entrance shouting insults, calling him a pig and a racist in front of the native women who were arriving for their luncheon. "I had to follow her all the way out to the street. She told me that I should get a lawyer because she was going to sue me for discrimination. Can she do that?" Klaus asks.

"No. The hotel is private property, and she was not an invited or welcome guest."

"None of the ladies knew who she was, and she insulted them when I hauled her out of there because she didn't get to finish her lunch. Fuckin' bitch." Klaus was offended by the struggle and he didn't care who heard it.

"Language," the manager cautions.

Gabi comes by to report that the housekeepers are fed up with the front desk renting rooms before check-in time.

"What's wrong with guests checking in early?" the manager asks.

"But not before we finish the rooms Sir." Gabi is put out that protocol has been breached.

"If we have rooms, we rent them. I don't care if it's seven in the morning. If people arrive you need to work around them."

"But they ask for things."

"Gabi." The manager leans forward to make a more intimate connection. There is a mutual respect between them, which sometimes turns flirtatious. "I truly admire your thoroughness and attention to detail, but you must remember that you are not working for the King of Sicily. This is a mid level hotel. I pay you by the hour. Handsomely. Make it work."

"The girls, they won't be happy." Gabi exits the office reluctantly.

Happy or not, the manager has no intention of letting inconvenience to his housekeeper's lose the hotel money because guests are not allowed to occupy their rooms before check in time. He heard that the weekend before, several of these early arrivals had stormed out and threatened never to return.

Tuesday

The night auditor's report indicates that he has again exceeded his mandate. The auditor, Fred, is a tall weedy man with glasses and a head that was mostly bald except for the wisps that grew too long on the back and sides. Fred had aspirations to be a policeman, or at minimum a security guard. He has been hired to process the accounts overnight and be present in case hotel guests have late night or early morning requests. The manager narrows his eyes and reads aloud the tightly scrawled handwritten report while Fred sits on the hard chair opposite.

"At 3:05am as I conducted my third security round, I saw a man standing at the traffic lights on the opposite side of the street. When I crossed the road to investigate his suspicious behaviour, he walked away from me in the direction of Balfour Street. I followed for two hundred meters down the main road and when I was satisfied that he no longer presented a danger to the hotel I returned to the office." Fred looks at the manager waiting to be complimented for his diligence. .

"You know that the hotel was robbed last night?" the manager asks.

"Yes Sir." The night auditor bows his head.

"And where were you?"

"On a security round Sir."

"All the way down at the next intersection? Fred, your duties don't go beyond the hotel property. And how did that guy on video manage to get the cash drawer open so easily? It looks to me like it wasn't locked."

"Maybe I forgot Sir."

"Forgot?" Angry and frustrated, the manager stands up from his desk with such force that his chair rolls back and knocks over a wastebasket. He kicks the metal wastebasket, and the crash fills up the small office. "You are here to do the accounts Fred! You of all people should know that 'maybe' is a word that doesn't figure in accounting or in security. As of tonight, you are forbidden to set foot off the hotel property. And if I discover you have left the cash unlocked again, that will be the end of your career as an auditor."

"Just trying to do my job Sir."

The manager dismisses Fred with a finger pointed toward the door.

Nora the front office manager reports that one of the front desk employees, Cecile, a Quebecois with a corseted Rubens body, has angered the other desk clerks with her constant eating. Not only does she eat in front of guests, but leaves the telephones, keyboards, desks and chairs covered in stickiness and crumbs. She keeps snacks in her purse, her coat, and in the pockets of her uniform jacket. Every time someone opens a desk drawer, they find cookies, pastry, nuts, mouldy fruit and half eaten sandwiches. The other employees object to spending the first half hour of their shifts cleaning up after her. Nora hasn't managed to get the message across because Cecile takes it as criticism of her size. The manager promises he will speak to her. Perhaps she is having emotional difficulties.

Klaus in Maintenance reports that kids playing in the elevator on the weekend have caused a mechanical problem and that now the elevator doesn't arrive exactly level at each floor. Several people have already tripped.

"We need to get this fixed right away." The manager calls the elevator company who will send somebody later, but the request turns unfriendly when the company tells him that nobody can come until later, which will need to be paid as overtime. He turns back to Klaus. "Did anyone put up caution signs?"

"I didn't see any Sir."

"Damn," the manager mutters to himself and calls the front desk to make warning signs for every floor. "We don't want any lawsuits." he says to Klaus.

"Yeah man," Klaus nods in puppy dog agreement. "Not like that guy yesterday."

"What guy? Yesterday?" The manager twists his neck to look at Klaus from the corner of his eye.

"The elevator doors closed on this little boy. His dad said he was going to take us to court."

"What? Nobody told me." The manager sits up straight in his chair.

"Nora says he calmed down later when they found out that the infra red beam on the doors was set higher than his son. Maybe his son ducked underneath it. Kids do that kind of shit."

"You should have told me. Are they still here?."

"No. They checked out the same night they checked in."

"Oh, jeez." It was the manager's turn to swear.

Wednesday

To justify spending half of her annual sales budget for a hotel convention in Orlando, Megan the sales director rattles off a torrent of empty superlatives about how profitable her upcoming trip to Florida will be for the hotel. The manager has doubts as Florida is on the opposite corner of the continent. He has also heard that Megan, a single mother, has promised to take her son to Disney World, which is conveniently located next door to Orlando. The manager needs to check with the hotel owners that he has permission to pay for the questionable expedition and to check with the franchise director for legitimacy. He doesn't want to hear excuses about how Megan will juggle her son's activities with the convention, so he doesn't bring up the subject, but he is cold with Megan, not happy with her for thinking she can outwit him. Her next step would probably be to ask for extra holidays, so she didn't have to rush home from the convention.

Klaus stops by the office to report that the pool problem has been resolved.

"What problem?" the manager asks.

"There was some water in the parking lot," Klaus hasn't fully entered the room. "It's gone now."

"What happened?" The manager calls after his shadow as it disappears behind the doorway. There is silence and then Klaus's head appears.

"The pool overflowed," he said. "No problem." He is gone again.

"Klaus!" the manager calls. "Come back here."

Again there is silence before Klaus takes a few timid steps and stands up to his full height, which fills the doorway.

"Why did the pool overflow?"

"I guess I forgot Sir."

"You left the water running?" The manager has seen this happen once already in the short time he had been there.

Klaus nods.

"For how long."

"All night Sir. It needed topping up, so I turned the water on, but when I was ready to leave, I got called to fix a toilet and I guess I forgot. Sorry."

Nora the front office manager is questioned about why the evening and night shifts didn't notice the water was running.

"Tiffany was on evenings," she explains, "and she's not a mechanical type." Tiffany is a girly girl who is more interested in the state of her hair and makeup than anything else around her. She often elicits a raised eyebrow from the manager for the number of buttons she has undone over her abundant cleavage, and has been reprimanded for sitting up on the front desk to chat with clients, who she insists on calling 'You Guys' no matter who they are. "She says that when she took her smoke break, she heard water running but thought it was a fountain."

"We don't have a fountain. How long has she worked here?" the manager asks.

"The guests really like her Sir."

"And why didn't Fred notice it last night?"

"Fred wrote in the logbook that he saw the water in the parking lot but that he was no plumber. He says you told him nothing outside the hotel building was his business. He wrote down a few times in the night where the water was going and how big the lake in the lot was getting."

The manager puts his head in his hands again.

"But I do have some good news for y' Sir," Nora has already figured out how to move on from the pool fiasco. "Sylvia Philips paid up. She came back with enough to cover her to the end of the month, and she gave the housekeepers a nice note to say thanks for being so patient and all. Made me feel a touch guilty for pestering her."

"How long is that woman going to stay here?" The manager asks rhetorically but Nora answers.

"She's always doubtful Sir. Says she'll let us know later."

The manager sighs. "And the other one? The welfare case?"

"Gone Sir. But he left a few things behind."

"Like what?"

"His girlfriend Sir."

"Did you call somebody? The women's shelter? Her mother? We need to get her out of here. Every night she's in that room we lose money. I don't suppose we saw any of that?"

Nora shakes her head to say no.

"Keep on it," the manager says. "The government put them here in the first place so the government can pay."

Nora is called away by the front desk to speak to a guest who has some complaints about her room. She is not gone long before she is back asking for the manager's help.

"This one has really gone nuts,'" she says.

The manager agrees to intervene before the situation gets out of hand. He is directed to the woman's room where two children are jumping on one bed and her husband is parked on the other bed watching television. The woman is adamant that not only did she find the toilet roll off the holder, but there was a dead fly on the window ledge, she was certain none of her group would be able to stay in the hotel.

The manager tries to calm her down, but she is too far gone into threats of calling the Chamber of Commerce and the Better Business Bureau to pay any attention to him. She wants to cancel her entire team's bookings rather than listen to any offers of upgrades or discounts. The manager accompanies her down to the lobby to arrange other rooms. On the way she continues to shout into his ear and as they stand waiting for the elevator, huffing like a bull, she begins to point on the elevator button. The manager chastises her for damaging hotel property, which only makes her hammer the controls harder. Before they arrive in the lobby, he has determined that she will not be staying at the hotel any longer than necessary.

At the front desk, Nora explains different room options but instead of helping resolve the situation, the woman calls her names that should not be repeated in front of children. The manager says that if the woman insists on cancelling her entire team's rooms at the last minute, the hotel will charge her for one night for one room as a late cancellation fee. Her refusal is adamant, loud, and verbally abusive.

When the manager has heard enough, he politely informs her that her language and behaviour are unacceptable and that she is not welcome to stay. Rather than tackle him, because he is taller than her, she reaches over the front desk and tries to slap Nora. The manager insists she leave the hotel immediately. There is more bad language. He threatens to call the police and she agrees, but when he picks up the phone, she tries to grab it out of his hand. As they wait for the police to arrive, it is discovered that the woman's husband, who has stood quietly in the lobby behind her, his arms crossed, not saying anything at all, is an off duty policeman in another city. He remains uninvolved but cooperative when the police escort the woman and her family to their car. Some of the parents that the woman hasn't been able to contact arrive for their rooms and are happy to stay, even after their hysterical friend contacts them and tells them to leave immediately. "She isn't good at coping with stress," one of them explains.

Thursday

Gabi the head housekeeper arrives in a panic because she has heard that a very pregnant woman and her husband have checked in the night before.

"What if she makes a birth on one of our beds?" Gabi is out of breath having run down the stairs from the fourth floor to tell the manager the news. "She should be in the hospital."

"It's probably not time yet," the manager reasons.

"But we don't want to see the time. We must get her out of here," Gabi begs.

"She's welcome like anyone else." The manager makes a calming gesture with both hands. "Almost anyone else. If you're worried about your bedding, offer them towels and sheets that aren't your first line linen. They won't know the difference at this point."

Gabi pauses, says "Hmm..." and walks out with a finger pressed to her cheekbone, knowing exactly what she will do. "Furbo," she says, not knowing that the manager understands some Italian.

The manager summons the front desk food nibbler Cecile to his office to hear what she has to say about her eating and hoarding habits. It is an unsatisfying exchange because Cecile apologizes repeatedly but offers no clues to the cause of her problem or what she might be doing to fix it. "My 'usband, he is a chef," is all she can come up with. As well as her hotel work Cecile is a cosmetics company saleswoman hoping to earn enough commissions for a pink Cadillac. Nora has already cautioned her about bringing her sales kit to work and casually mentioning her sideline to guests when they check in. The manager has also heard that she neglects her front desk duties to assemble bridal books for Megan the sales director, hoping to be appointed the official hotel wedding consultant, even though there is no such position.

When they sit down to talk, the manager requests that she restrict her consumption to break times, that she eats out of sight of guests and that she cleans up the area around her when she is done. "We don't like a sticky office," he says.

After a litany of "forgive me Father" apologies from her, and a promise to do better, the manager doesn't see any indication that her behaviour will change.

"Perhaps you are right," she says, "Maybe I should eat in the restaurant, so I won't bring so much from home."

The manager has seen enough half empty restaurant plates around the front desk to know that her solution might make the problem worse.

Nora requests a meeting with the manager to discuss an incident from the previous evening involving a group of Red Cross nurses who had rooms booked through the Mobile Blood Bank. Nurses are usually good guests who aren't out getting drunk every evening and vomiting on the furniture, so it was unusual there had been a problem.

"I know they did it on purpose." Nora's cheeks are flushed. "Just to get me on the floor. One of them, the bleach blond woman, is a right crooked piece of work. The kinda person you want to give a smack to out behind the shed."

"Slow down and tell me what happened." The manager leans back in his chair.

"These nurses had three rooms and all six of them came at once, fulla themselves and insisting on things. The Red Cross pays for their rooms so it shoulda been easy, but one of them kept asking me about breakfast.

How much does it cost? Depends what ya eat I told her. She kept on at me until something from my nan just jumped out of my head. "How long is a piece of string?" I said. Them others fell about laughing but missy didn't like it. Wasn't five minutes later when I get this call from her room saying that I need to get up there right away because there's a big problem. All of them are there standing around the bathroom door pointing at this one curly black hair on the floor like it was some tarantula looking ta jump."

The manager winces. These things happen sometimes. If a housekeeper is in a hurry and doesn't look back over her work, details get missed. He once had a guest who insisted that she couldn't stay in her room because there was semen on the wall. Housekeepers were sent to investigate and found a few spots of a transparent dried substance on the oak headboard but were hard pressed to understand why the woman assumed it was semen. They cleaned, but the guest still refused to stay there.

"Okay," Nora continues. "So, I picked up the hair with a tissue and flushed it, but no that wasn't good enough. I had to go down to the laundry for a bucket and sponge and clean the floor all over again with them nurses from hell standing over me. I'm sure they did it just to let me know they are superior. You'd think they got enough by sucking out people's blood all day."

"Sorry you had to do that. " the manager commiserates. "I'll ask Gabi to pay more attention so it doesn't happen again, but I think Gabi secretly likes the idea of you desk people on your hands and knees scrubbing floors."

"She can keep it," Nora's bottom lip turns down. "I've done enough of that at me mutter's cafe back home on the Rock."

As she is on the way out the door, she remembers to tell the manager that Cecile had come to her in tears after her interview about food. "She was too ashamed to tell you that she was one of nine kids and they never had enough to eat."

"That's a feeble excuse," the manager says. "Tell her it's time to grow up and take responsibility for herself," but he was already distracted by an online review from the father whose boy had a problem with the elevator. It wasn't good, but it didn't mention lawsuits.

A bus tour arrives unexpectedly in the evening looking to occupy their rooms for a night on their expedition through Western Canada. Nobody knows anything about their booking. Nora calls Megan who is at a Chamber of Commerce wine tasting party. She remembers the booking but says that the oversight is the fault of the front desk who must have misplaced her booking request. Nora is spitting nails and trying to be polite to the guests who are French and completely fill the lobby with their lilting accents and waving hands. Nora is a professional and blithely explains that most of the group will be staying at the hotel but that a few people will be walked to another hotel. Some guests object to walking anywhere at the end of their long day, but Nora remembers that she has been using hotel-speak and that "walk" was an expression that means transported.

Transported? They looked at each and begin muttering about trains and planes, until Nora qualifies herself with the magic word, taxi. Ah. Taxi. Everyone knows that. How far? Five minutes? D'accord. There were a few mutterings of "mal organisé" but the group are too tired to resist.

Friday

With no mention to the manager about the previous night's oversight, Megan stops by to report that she has had an inquiry to book two banquet rooms and thirty hotel rooms for a weekend in August. The clients are willing to pay the going seasonal rate, but the event is for a national meet-up of bondage and discipline group who wish to hold seminars. They have stated that their meetings are not open to the public but that they hope other guests will not be offended by their unusual choice of attire as the participants make their way between their rooms and the seminars. Does the manager know if the banquet rooms are soundproof? The answer to Megan is no on all counts.

Fred has written in his report about an incident the previous evening. Just after midnight he checks in a man and woman who arrive unexpectedly at the front desk. He is under the impression they are not tourists because they arrive in a taxi and have no suitcases. The manager can guess what is coming, either a rental by the hour or a drug deal, both of which he strongly discourages. He has tried to educate his staff to be wary of cash paying local residents without luggage, but these warning signals had passed Fred's misplaced defences easily enough.

"They were in their room less than fifteen minutes," Fred has written in his night shift log, "when the man ran into the lobby half dressed and holding up his pants, shouting 'That bitch stole my wallet, that bitch stole my wallet.' He looked behind the lobby pillars and doors for her but she must have already been gone. I offered to call the police, but he told me to mind my own business. Luckily, he paid for the room when he arrived."

"I should damn well hope so," the manager says when he finishes reading the account and spends an hour of his afternoon going back and forth through Tuesday's video surveillance to discover that the person who stole the front desk cash had arrived on foot, unrecognizable under a hoodie. There isn't a single usable image that can be sent to the police. The money is lost with no hope of recovery or even the likelihood of catching the thief. There is a strong possibility the thief would try again since the first time has been so easy, so the manager issues a sharp and sarcastic communiqué about keeping the cash drawer locked.

The manager sees an ambulance pull up at the hotel front door but doesn't know why. Sometimes an ambulance pulls up to drop off a crew member who is taking a first aid course at the hotel, but this one has its lights flashing. He calls the front desk, but nobody answers. As he stands up from his desk to go down to the lobby, Gabi arrives out of breath, flustered, and pale, pleased to announce that the baby who had been threatening to mess up her linen had been born and is fine. The mother and paramedics agreed not to cut the cord right away so some of her precious linen was saved. Mother and baby about to go to the hospital, and though there is a bit of cleaning up to do, a sense of wonder and accomplishment pervades the hotel.

"It was like the birth of Jesus." Gabi's eyes fill with tears and she turns away shaking her head as she leaves the office to get on with her duties.

At the front desk, Tiffany has already blown up balloons and hung them from the lobby pictures; she can't wait to tell everyone who passes by the happy news, and is making signs announcing the birth. The manager tells her to take down the signs and balloons and have some respect for guest privacy. She doesn't hide the dirty look she gives him.

Saturday

The reports from Friday evening indicate that a couple of soccer teams that checked in all together and overwhelmed Tiffany who was at the front desk by herself. Apparently, she fled from behind the desk in tears, leaving the guests flabbergasted and blaming each other. After a cigarette and some gentle reassurance from one of the soccer moms she recovered enough to start on the list of requests. Four rooms want cots, six want extra towels, three claim they have light bulbs burned out, two families want to have a barbecue, three have complaints about their air conditioners, one mother needs to know where she can get her son's cleats fixed. Tiffany had asked Klaus to stay late to help with the wave of demands, and she hopes he will be paid overtime because that was the only condition on which he agreed to work late.

Nora is the one to inform the manager that Sylvia Phillips has died, and that an ambulance would be arriving soon to take her body away. The housekeepers reported that she was already cold so there was no reason for hurry or alarm.

Nobody had seen Sylvia since she came back from her lawyers a few days earlier. The housekeepers usually visited her once a week to change the linen, restock the bathroom and check the condition of the room. This time she didn't answer the door, and when they used their master key, they found her body on the floor between the bathroom and the bed. The bed had been slept in, but she hadn't made it to the bathroom in time. Gabi wasn't working that morning, so the housekeepers ran to the front desk who called the police. Nobody thought that foul play was involved, and though no particular illness had ever been mentioned, Sylvia was so thin and pale that one could believe that she starved herself to death. The manager guessed that this might have been her plan all along. She didn't want to do it at home too close to the prying concerns of her parents. They might have found her at home, and she didn't want to be found by them.

Sunday

Sunday is a check-out day, when soccer, baseball, and lacrosse families limp back to their cars after a weekend of partying and games. Once the teams have left and calm has descended on the hotel, there is a new industriousness without guests underfoot. The staff have a chance to bring the hotel back to a clean and serene state, ready for the few arrivals of the evening. Sunday night guests are corporate or salespeople starting their week in another town ready to hit the street on Monday. They are pharmaceutical representatives, lawyers who have to be in the city for the court cases, or construction workers building the new bridge who return to the hotel after their weekends off, and a few genuine tourists from every corner of the world.

One guest from an unexpected quarter arrives that Sunday. The manager has stopped at the hotel on his day off to retrieve a set of keys. When he crosses the lobby, he hears his name mentioned in a questioning tone by a woman his own height wearing a man's fedora. When she removes the hat, her fine blonde hair falls free and makes an electrified halo around her head. He recognizes the ex-wife who he hasn't seen in twenty years. He thinks of Bogart in Casablanca saying, "Of all the gin joints in all the towns in all the world, she walks into mine," but that is another story.

The End